"From Joey's initial problem, every page is engrossing. As Joey gets deeper into trouble, the reader gets deeper into the story. This is a read-it-under-the-covers-by-flashlight book. It is very hard to put down. The author is true to her subject; Joey is never false. His is a memorable story."—*Young Readers' Review*

"The appealing subject of guide-dog training enriches this vital story of a boy's many difficult adjustments to life in a new community. Skillful writing and depth of understanding."—*Horn Book*

"Joey Van Oolbekink, who recently moved to Oregon, finds life in the suburb much different from life on the Iowa farm. Joey's new life is complicated by his old fashioned parents. *A Dog for Joey* is well worth reading and may open some horizons for children who have 'problem' parents."—*Elementary English*

"With the arrival of a puppy, Joey's whole life changes. He learns about friendship, both human and canine, and more important, the difference between selfishness and love. Nan Gilbert tells the story with sympathy and understanding."—Galesburg *Register-Mail*

Other Books by Nan Gilbert

ooooooooooooooooooooooo

CHAMPIONS DON'T CRY

THE UNCHOSEN

A DOG
FOR
JOEY

○○○○○○○○○○

Nan Gilbert

○○○○○○○○○○○○○○○○○○○○○○○○○○○○

A DOG
FOR
JOEY

A HARPER TROPHY BOOK

HARPER & ROW, PUBLISHERS

New York, Evanston, San Francisco, London

To our once and always friends:
Djikki I and II
Texas Duke
Texas Rio
and her puppies: Lone Star, Ranger, Tornado, Cowboy,
Black Gold, Tessie, and Bluebonnet, who is our
Bebe,
and to
Hans,
this book is lovingly dedicated

Acknowledgment

ooooooooooooooooooooooooooo

Special appreciation is due Guide Dogs for the Blind, Inc., of San Rafael, California, whose fine non-profit service to the blind inspired this book, and whose assistance materially helped in its writing.

N.G.

I

ooooooooo

The
Quarrel

1

ooooooooo

"I WON'T DO IT," muttered Joey. "I don't have to! He can't make me!"

Stout words, but Joey didn't say them very loudly. In fact, he didn't say them at all till he was already outside the gate and on his way, the sack of Westport *Journal*s in his bicycle basket, the hated red wagon bouncing and bumping behind him.

For the truth was (as Joey knew very well), he did have to lug the wagonload of fresh garden vegetables with him and offer the produce for sale at houses along his newspaper route. His father had said so. . . .

And in the Van Oolbekink household, his father's word was law. Not even his mother argued with Dirk Van Oolbekink! As for his brothers, grown men though they were, they had done just as they were told right up to the day Dirk signed over the farm to them and left Iowa to settle in Oregon.

Joey swerved sharply. He zigzagged back and forth across the quiet suburban road. No use. The wagon remained firmly attached. What else?—when Dirk himself had tied the knots.

"Boy!" an indignant voice called after him.

3

"Stop that! You're scattering vegetables over the road!"

Joey didn't stop nor look back. He bent low over his handlebars and scooted out of the vicinity in the straightest possible line. He'd recognized the voice; it was Mrs. Wickshire, prickliest of the neighborhood thorns. Prick, stickle, jab—that's all she'd done since Joey's arrival eight mortally long weeks ago!

At first Joey had been relieved to find no boys his age, only elderly couples, living in the neighborhood where Dirk had purchased their new home. Joey distrusted "town" boys. Back home his friends had all come from nearby farms. They had attended the same consolidated school on a country crossroads, and when they went into town with their families on Saturday night, they had immediately sought each other out to band together like wary tourists on foreign soil.

Now here he was, living in town himself!—well, anyway, on the edge of town. In September he'd even have to go to a town school. At the thought, Joey scowled. He expected nothing good from Hopkins Junior High.

Glumly he pedaled toward the outlying district that had been assigned him by the *Journal* manager.

"Not too big a route," Mr. Landers had admitted

4

cheerfully, "but the only one available right now. You do a good job, Joey, and I'll give you first chance at something better when it opens up."

"Shucks," thought Joey, "who wants a *Journal* route anyway?" As short a time as he'd lived in Westport, Joey already knew that a *Morning Star* route was far superior. *Star* carriers not only earned more, but made their deliveries long before breakfast, leaving their after-school hours free for fun. "I wouldn't mind getting up that early," Joey told himself wistfully.

On the farm he had always been up before daylight to help with the chores. He'd liked the big barn at that hour. Even on subzero mornings he hadn't minded the quick dash across hard-packed, squeaking snow, through air so icy it burned his lungs. The barn would be warm and steamy from the animals' soft breathing. They'd turn their heads to look at him from gentle, brooding brown eyes; for a moment the peculiar quiet would wrap them all about, boy and beast alike, laying a spell over them, bidding them *hush . . . wait . . . listen.*

"Hey!" a boy's voice hailed him. "You're losin' stuff outa your wagon!"

Another bicyclist was coming down the road toward him. Joey bent still lower, pedaled still faster, letting the rackety din of the wagon serve as excuse

5

for his apparent deafness. In a moment he'd be even with the boy, in another moment, safely past. . . .

A black-and-white-and-brown object came out from a clump of bushes and shot across the road almost under Joey's front wheel. Joey braked to a panic stop, but the wagon kept on going. *Crash!*—it whanged into his rear wheel. Bicycle, wagon, and Joey spilled onto the road.

The other bicyclist skidded to a stop.

"Tex!" he yelled after the vanishing object. "Whatcha think you're *doin'?* . . . Gosh, I'm sorry!" The boy bent anxiously over Joey. "When that dog smells a rabbit, he goes nuts! You hurt?"

"Naw," mumbled Joey. Furious at being made to look clumsy before this stranger, he scrambled to his feet. His jeans were stained and dusty; squashed vegetables littered the road around him. "Darn ol' dog!"

The cause of his humiliation—a portly beagle with graying muzzle—returned from his unprofitable chase to sniff Joey's jeans with lively interest. Sullenly Joey shoved him away. "G'wan, beat it, you mutt!"

"Hey now, wait a minute!" The beagle's owner, who had been scooping up the least damaged vegetables, paused to protest. "Maybe he's a pest sometimes, but Tex is no mutt!"

"Yeh? Who says?"

6

"The American Kennel Club, that's who says!" The boy dumped his armload of vegetables in the wagon with indignant emphasis. "Tex is a registered purebred beagle!"

"Real great!"

"You're darn right! He's got a pedigree *this* long, an' nine champions in his ancestry!"

"Huh!" scoffed Joey. "I'll bet!"

"Okay, look him up yourself in the AKC stud book! Texas Gay Bugler the third, that's who you're shovin'!"

"Well, goody for me!" retorted Joey. He slammed his bike back on its wheels, replaced the sack of *Journal*s with a thump, and scowling ferociously, streaked away from the smear of tomatoes on the road.

"Let that smart-aleck kid clean 'em up!" he told himself. "Him an' his fancy dog! Pedigree . . . champion ancestors—chee, way he acted, you'd think his ol' hound was a crown prince or something! Loud mouth. Show-off. Big shot."

Squeak-rattle-bumpity-clang went the wagon. A taunting sound. Suddenly it was just too much to take. Joey's pride, as well as his body, had been tumbled in the dust.

Angrily Joey flung himself off his bike and yanked loose the knots that coupled him to his wagon. "There, that'll shut you up!" he growled. "Stupid ol' wagon!"

But he couldn't just leave it sitting here. Some busybody like that kid with the dog was sure to spot it and come hot-footing after him to tell him he'd lost it! Joey looked around him.

He was just passing the House. That was the name Joey had assigned to the place since the day his *Journal* route had brought it to his attention. The House was set well back from the road, screened by heavy-limbed old walnut trees. Its wide lawns—luxuriant with flowering shrubs and rose borders, and dotted with game courts—stretched out to meet the road. Along the far edge, bordered by a tangle of blackberry bushes, lay a still pond where ducks paddled in the sunset-tinted water.

In all the weeks Joey had been delivering *Journals*, the House had appeared untenanted. Nobody played croquet or tennis or badminton on its courts; nobody picked the lush roses or fed the quacking ducks; and whoever kept the grass mowed to a green velvet carpet did so before Joey appeared on the scene.

Joey shot a quick glance up and down the road. No car, no bicyclist, no pedestrian in sight. Swiftly he shoved the hated red wagon deep into the blackberry thicket.

Relief at being free of the burden lightened Joey's heart as it lightened his load. Now he was no different from any other newspaper carrier. With smooth efficiency he rolled his *Journal*s as he pedaled along and deftly poked each roll into the proper cylinder below the mailboxes—green for the local *Journal*, gray for the big-city *Star*.

Next year, Joey planned, he'd be putting his papers in the gray cylinders. Maybe even this fall a *Star* route would open up, and the manager would call him, saying, "You still interested in the *Star*, Joey? I've been hearing fine things about you! Landers says you're the best carrier he's got!"

More than pride drove Joey toward a *Star* route. From the *Journal* he earned less than four dollars a month—not nearly enough for a boy going into junior high. But if he complained about it at home, Dirk would say, "Plenty of jobs for a good strong boy who keeps his eyes open!" Or, more likely, "Better work a little harder to sell those vegetables! That money's all yours, you know; I don't ask a cent of it."

Chee! Joey bet he'd be the only kid at Hopkins Junior High who didn't get an allowance. Old-country square, that's what Pa was!

Back home it hadn't been too serious a problem. Most of his friends were in the same fix. They too had

9

parents like Dirk and Anna Van Oolbekink, a generation or less away from Holland, parents who still maintained the strict rules by which they themselves had been raised.

But out here things were different. Out here *he'd* be different, and alone in his difference. Trouble, that's what lay ahead of him in this foreign town, this foreign school—just plain trouble!

His basket was empty of *Journal*s. The sun had set. Now the quick twilight of hill country shadowed the sky. On his way home, Joey stopped reluctantly at the blackberry thicket to retrieve his wagon. Dirk would frown at the heap of unsold vegetables. And Joey would mutter, as he had other times: "Not my fault if folks'd rather buy their stuff at a store."

The wagon was where he'd left it, but Joey stared aghast at its contents. Squirrels or birds or ducks had found it a treasure trove. Tomatoes were pecked open, corn stripped and shelled by sharp teeth, carrots bitten off!

"Goshamighty!" Joey cried in dismay. It was one thing to haul home a wagon almost as full as when he left, but quite another to explain *this* mess!

Whatever could he say? Could he say a big kid had picked a fight with him—pelted him with his own vegetables? (But then he'd get a licking for fighting; Pa wouldn't care *who* started it.)

10

Okay, he'd say he left the wagon on the road while he delivered a little old lady's *Journal* to her door. (And why, Pa would scold, hadn't he taken the wagon with him so he could offer the little old lady some nice fresh vegetables?)

She didn't buy from peddlers, Joey would answer; there was a sign on her gate said so. (And in the minute it took to run to her door, all this gnawing and nibbling and pecking had been done?)

"Chee!" said Joey helplessly. While he stood here fussing and fretting, the twilight was deepening to charcoal dusk. Anna would be waiting supper. Dirk would be looking severely at the clock. Every minute he wasted compounded his problems. *What was he to do?*

Impulsively he upended the wagon. *Splash!* went corn and carrots and tomatoes into the pond, triggering a chorus of startled quacks from the drowsing ducks. At the same moment lights sprang to life in the House. A door slammed; a dog barked. "Somebody out there?" a man's voice sang out.

Joey didn't pause to tie the wagon to his bicycle rack. Hanging on to the rope, the wagon swaying and jouncing beside him, Joey hurtled rackety-bounce toward home.

11

2

OOOOOOOOO

WHEN DIRK'S DOCTOR had advised him the previous winter to move to a milder climate, decisions had to be made firmly and promptly. Joey's two older brothers would take over the farm. Dirk junior was about to be married; the young couple would share the big farmhouse with Teunis. But Joey, deemed too young to be left behind in spite of his passionate protests, would go with his parents to Oregon.

As soon as school was out, the move was made. The house Dirk senior bought for them on the outskirts of Westport was an older place surrounded by half an acre of high-fenced yard.

"Plenty of room for a garden," Dirk said with satisfaction.

"We will raise our potatoes and green stuff," Anna planned happily. "Just like home."

To Joey, Number 760 Orchard Lane was about as much like home as an Eskimo igloo or an Arab tent! Grumpy with loneliness, he went out to survey his new surroundings.

The neighborhood first. Old houses, big yards

much like their own, deeply shaded by huge old trees. The people he saw all matched their houses—old, graying, slightly bent, a little in need of repairs.

Then the town. Not really very large, but looking like a metropolis compared to the small farming community Joey had come from.

Last of all, the school most likely to gobble him up in September. HOPKINS JUNIOR HIGH—the gold letters of its name glinted in the sun. A daunting structure with a bewildering number of wings and ells. Joey hurried past, head down, hands instinctively tightening into fists. A town school—*chee!* What would Johnny and Claus and Benny, his friends at home, think of *that!*

Glumly Joey had found his way back to Orchard Lane. He was just passing the house next door to their own when he saw a tiny white-haired lady standing on tiptoe to peer over the fence into their yard.

Sensing his curious stare, she swung around to frown at him severely. "Young man, just what does your father think he's doing?"

What Dirk was doing proved that he too had been to town. He had rented a rototiller and was plowing up their yard, his neat straight furrows making no detour for flower beds or small shrubs.

The little lady at the fence gasped in horror.

13

"Dear, oh, dear, there goes poor Mrs. Crowther's iris border! And her prize peony—oh, I can't bear to watch!" Nimbly she climbed onto the bottom fence rail for a better view. "Not her roses too; this is awful, simply awful! Mr. Crowther should have known better than to sell to *barbarians!*"

Joey slunk past the angry figure, then plunged for the safety of his own front door. "What's Pa doin', for Pete's sake?" he exploded. "Plowin' up the whole place—"

Anna was unpacking, trying to fit items from home into the strange shape of new rooms. "Not the whole place," she soothed Joey. "Just enough for a nice garden. Maybe a few chickens—"

"Chickens!" Joey yelped. "Nobody keeps chickens in town! Golly moses, ya want us to look like—like *barbarians?"*

"What's all this racket?" demanded Dirk, appearing at the back door. "Joey, where did you run off to when there was work to be done? Get into your overalls and come break up clods. The soil looks good," he added to Anna. "A little tired, maybe. Tomorrow we will spread a load of manure . . ."

"Creeps!" muttered Joey and slam-banged out of the room. Manure! Well, that ought to drive the little old lady off her fence! Off her rocker too! Here they'd only just arrived, and already people wished

14

they'd stayed home!

Well, so did Joey. And he'd get back there too, he promised himself—sooner than soon. Just see if he didn't!

Anna had spread her patchwork quilts on the beds, her crocheted tidies on couch and chairs, her braided rag rugs on the floors. The big Bible and family picture album appeared on the parlor table, and the tea set that had belonged to Anna's own mother took its familiar place on the sideboard. Little by little the strange rooms acquired a look of home.

The ruined lawn greened over again, this time with leaf-lettuce and beet tops and lacy carrot fronds, all tended as carefully as the neighbors' flower beds. Nor did any chickens appear to spoil the picture. The peppery little lady next door put a stop to that, sternly invoking a zoning law before Anna's idea had got beyond a roll of chicken wire and a few rough boards.

Anna accepted her disappointment quickly. "Such work chickens make," she said. "It will be good not to have a henhouse to clean, eh, Joey?"

But Joey wouldn't yet admit there was *anything* good about Westport. He held tight to his dream of getting back to the farm, to his brothers and friends, to the surroundings he knew and loved.

Even securing a *Journal* route didn't change his

15

mind, though he was secretly a little proud of his sortie into the newspaper offices. Nobody had gone with him, nobody had even known what he planned to do. Locating the addresses and making his application at the two offices had been entirely his own project.

Dirk had made no secret of *his* pleasure in Joey's accomplishment. "Now the boy shows a little gumption!" he had told Anna.

The first requirement of the new job, of course, had been a bicycle. Dirk had gone downtown with Joey to help him find the very best bargain in a used bike. After Joey had counted out the price from his little hoard of savings, Dirk had said, "Next we will go to the bank. It is time you had a savings account. A businessman doesn't keep his earnings in a peanut-butter jar; he invests them where they will work for him."

The savings-account book added inches to Joey's stature. He tucked it away in his top dresser drawer beside the peanut-butter jar where he would still put incoming cash until the next deposit date.

The garden sprouted richly under Dirk's skillful hands, not hurt in the least by the daily disapproving survey of Mrs. Wickshire next door. To Joey the vegetables meant only hours of tedious weeding and hoeing and watering. . . .

Till the day Dirk announced his plan to have

Joey sell the surplus door-to-door.

"Good business training," said Dirk, paying no heed to Joey's dismay, "and more money for the bank account." He himself purchased the red wagon from a rummage shop and supervised its first loading.

"*Na, na,* the radishes in a bouquet—like this, see? And scrub the carrots, don't just hose them . . . *ach,* Anna, the boy will never make a storekeeper, that much is plain!"

Nor a salesman either, Dirk might have added as the skimpy profits of Joey's new undertaking trickled in. How Joey hated knocking on strangers' doors and offering his wares!

"Want 'ny vegetables?" he'd mumble, so sure of the answer that he was already turning away on the last word.

Some days, especially after a busy housewife gave him an answer as short as his sales talk, Joey couldn't force himself to knock at any more doors. Then the only sales he made were to former customers who happened to be in their yards when he rattled past. "Joey!" somebody might hail him. "Do you have any nice tomatoes today?"

But though Joey kept his selling efforts to a minimum, he couldn't escape the bouncing red wagon, forever reminding him of the duty he was shirking.

17

That is, he didn't escape it till the August afternoon when he revolted and freed himself from its rackety torment—

Only to come back and find his problems redoubled.

3

ooooooooo

"GOLLY MOSES!" Joey fretted, streaking down the shadowy road, the empty wagon now swinging outward, now banging into his wheels. "What'm I gonna tell Pa?"

Dirk was in the carport, cleaning his garden tools, when Joey came rattling up the drive.

"You are late," said Dirk. "What took you so long?"

All the way home Joey had braced himself for that very question. Now here it was, and he still had no answer.

"Uh—well—what happened was—"

But Dirk's glance had gone beyond Joey to the empty wagon. Surprise and pleasure lightened the severe lines of his face. "Well, now, that is more like it! Anna," he called, "come see what the boy has done! Sold all he set out with. Yes, down to the last carrot!"

Anna appeared in the doorway, wiping her hands on her apron. "*Ach,* isn't that fine?" She beamed. "You'll see yet what a businessman the boy is!"

"Hey—" Joey tried to protest. But words deserted him.

"Put the money away now, Joey," his father directed, "and wash up for supper. The jar gets pretty heavy, *yah?* Soon now, we must go to the bank."

"Ulp!" choked Joey, and fled up the stairs. Now what was he to do?

From the back of a dresser drawer Joey brought out his money jar and shook it dismally. Though Dirk never asked how much he'd saved, Joey knew he kept close track of his earnings. Any day at all he could probably guess the total in the jar within ten or fifteen cents.

Or the total that *should* be in the jar!

Perspiration popped out on Joey's forehead. "Gee, why didn't I jus' bring the stuff home?" he mourned. Sure, Pa would've been mad. But nowhere near like he'd be now, adding lies and trickery to the sum of Joey's sins!

"Joey! Supper is on the table."

"Yeh, Ma, I'm comin'."

How much would Pa figure he'd earned this afternoon? As Joey washed his hands and splashed cold water on his steamy face he tried to calculate the lowest reasonable amount. A full wagonload! *Chee!* Even if he'd given away the smaller stuff—just good business, Pa said, to give a customer something extra—he should have made anyway two dollars.

Two dollars! A horrific sum. If the jar was all that amount short when they emptied it at the bank . . .

"JOEY!"

"Yeh, Pa!"

It was a sober, very worried boy who took his place at the table moments later. Every approving word and smile from Dirk and Anna increased Joey's guilt.

"Eat up now." Lovingly Anna heaped Joey's plate. "Your favorite cornbread and sausage!"

"Give the boy more sausage," Dirk directed. "Meat, that's what a hard-working man needs."

Joey tried to swallow a bite of cornbread; it stuck in his throat. "Too dry," he muttered.

"What a dummox I am," his mother cried, "forgetting the syrup! Wait, I get it."

"The good syrup, *yah?*" Dirk suggested. "To-night we will have the maple."

The shining cruet of pure maple syrup was re-served for distinguished company, like the minister. In growing dismay Joey watched the pale golden stream flood his plate as Anna tilted the pitcher. This was awful. Much more of this hero treatment and he'd be sick, right here at the table. Or bawl and blurt out who knows what? He had to start an argument, do *something* to get out from under this undeserved halo.

Impulsively he burst out, "Hey, c'n I have a dog? Alla kids 'round here got dogs. *Why* can't I have a dog?"

He knew what the answer would be. He knew Dirk's feelings about animals that served merely as household pets.

So did Anna. She said quickly, "*Ach,* you know there is no work here for a dog."

"Who says there isn't? He could be a watchdog, couldn't he? Nobody'd dare steal from a house where there was a good watchdog."

It wasn't like Joey to be so belligerent. Anna looked anxiously from father to son as she answered, "*Na, na,* Joey, it's like your pa says—a good lock on the door is cheaper and needn't be fed."

"Well, *I* need a dog!" The subject, brought up only to start an argument, had taken deeper hold of Joey. His spirit was still bruised from his encounter with the stranger who had shown such unreasonable pride in his dog. If Joey had a dog, *he* could brag too! "Gee, I pract'ly break my neck fallin' over dogs on my route," he insisted obstinately. "A dog of my own'd keep those mutts from botherin' me."

Anna looked increasingly anxious, but tonight

Dirk couldn't be provoked. He greeted Joey's outburst with rumbling laughter.

"What the boy needs is a water pistol and some of your vinegar, Anna! *Yah,* dogs won't bother you, once they smell your ma's vinegar."

"That's not what I mean at *all!* You don't know what you're talkin' about!"

"Joey!" Anna's glance pleaded with Dirk for patience. "The boy is tired . . ."

"And reason enough," Dirk said forgivingly, "after a good day's work. Eat your supper now, Joey, and get to bed early."

"Gee, you don't have to talk like I'm two years old or somethin'! All I wanta know is why I can't have a dog!"

Anna's hands trembled as she laid down knife and fork. She dreaded arguments and was always quick to serve as family peacemaker. Now, though, she could find nothing to say.

Dirk was silent too as he helped himself deliberately to more cornbread and sausage and syrup. Then he said, "Well, now, we talk about it another time, *yah?* Anna, what are you hiding out there in the kitchen? It smells like—"

"Apple cake!" In vast relief Anna hurried to set on the dessert. "Dutch apple cake, just as you like it with clotted cream!"

"And a wedge of cheese? Ah, here's food to stick to a man's ribs! Give the boy a good helping, Anna."

"CHEE!" Joey could stand no more. He pushed back from the table so violently that his chair tipped over. Out of the room and up the stairs he ran, and slammed his door—*crash!*—behind him.

4

OOOOOOOOO

JOEY LAY ON his bed, listening, almost hoping, for a footstep on the stairs and Dirk's stern voice. A sharp scolding would clear the air and make him feel less guilty. In fact, if the scolding was brisk enough, he might even blurt out the truth of his afternoon's misadventure. For if Pa was already riled about one thing, he might as well be mad about everything and get it over with!

But nobody followed Joey. Nobody ordered him back to set his chair straight and apologize and next time close the door quietly.

"Gollygee," whispered Joey, his mind churning, "what'm I gonna *do?*"

For a small interval he was safe. His crime wouldn't come to light till the next deposit day—but when would that be? "Soon," Pa had said. Soon might mean next week, or in a couple of days, or . . .

Tomorrow!

Joey was still awake, lying wide-eyed and alert in the darkness, when the creak of stair treads, a low mumble of voices, told him his parents were coming

25

up to bed. Quickly he rolled under the covers, just before Anna opened his door.

"Leave the boy be," he heard Dirk mutter.

"*Yah*, sure, I'll just look once and see if he is covered . . ."

"*Ach*, you baby him, Anna!"

The little exchange was nightly routine, Anna's one defiance of Dirk's wishes. Now she tiptoed into Joey's room. Joey closed his eyes and reminded himself to breathe slowly and deeply. He felt Anna's hand on his forehead (Anna had never owned a thermometer; touch was her only gauge of a child's temperature); feather-light, her lips brushed his cheek. Then her soft footsteps retreated, the door closed.

And Joey popped straight up in bed. His frantically darting mind had come upon an opening in the maze. As though Anna's touch had triggered a camera, Joey had seen a clear, instant picture of the object that might save him . . .

The big cracked teapot on the top kitchen shelf!

Back home the teapot had held Anna's egg-money; sale of fresh eggs was her own personal source of income. Out here there was no egg-money, yet the old teapot retained its familiar position on the top shelf. What did it hold? Trading stamps?

Grocery money?

"I'd only need it a day or so," Joey told himself.

Surely in that time he could make up the shortage in his money jar somehow. He'd find lawns to mow, he'd sell his football, he'd—oh, there were lots of ways, but they all needed time. And time—if Dirk should decide to go to the bank tomorrow—was what Joey didn't have.

But if in the meantime he could borrow from the teapot, surely Ma wouldn't miss two dollars before he'd had a chance to put it back!

Joey slid noiselessly out of bed. Heart beating so loudly he was afraid it would wake his parents, he inched open his door. The dark hall was eerily silent. A creaking board under his bare feet snapped like a firecracker. Joey froze motionless, not even breathing, till he was sure it had gone unheard. Step by stealthy step he edged down the stairs . . . across the dining room . . . into the kitchen.

With his finger on the light switch, Joey remembered that the kitchen was directly below his parents' bedroom. Should they hear the click of the switch, glance out the window, and see the lighted rectangle on the lawn—

No, he couldn't take the chance.

Groping his way in darkness, Joey climbed onto the counter and opened the cupboard door. He was thankful for Ma's tidy habit of arranging things just so and never changing their position. Now his hands went directly to the exact spot where the teapot should be standing. Without a fumble they closed on its cool surface and brought it down to the counter.

Yes, he'd guessed right! The teapot held money. Coins (he was very careful not to rattle them) and some bills. Joey would have preferred to take coins, but fishing out dimes and quarters and nickels was too risky. A coin dropped and rolling would sound louder than a thunderclap! Anyway, there were enough bills, so two less wouldn't shout their absence at Ma's first glance.

Carefully Joey separated two bills from the little roll. Noiselessly he replaced the teapot and closed the cupboard door. Quiet as a shadow he eased back up the stairs . . .

To the safety of his own room.

"Wow!" he whispered. The expedition had tired him more than a day's work at harvest time. Perspiration dampened his forehead; his hands trembled as he slid open his dresser drawer and tucked the bills deep down beside the money jar.

Making his weary way back to bed, Joey stumbled. His bare toes connected with a shoe, left just where he'd taken it off. The shoe crashed into a table leg; a book on top fell over on its side with a loud slap—

And roused nobody.

"Chee!" murmured Joey. His muscles twitched as he sank onto the bed. "Boy, I'll never do *that* again! Never in a hundred million trillion years."

The next morning, before going down to breakfast, Joey opened his dresser drawer to put the bills in his money jar. One bore a wrinkled, well-worn likeness of George Washington.

The other crisper, newer bill showed a less familiar portrait, Alexander Hamilton. Joey stared at it in disbelieving horror.

It was a ten-dollar bill.

5

ooooooooo

THAT DAY WAS surely the longest in Joey's life.

He could only pretend to eat breakfast. How could he swallow when at any moment Anna might look into the teapot and cry, "Help! Burglars! Dirk, we have been robbed!"

His garden work was so aimless that by noon he was still hoeing the first row. If Dirk so much as cleared his throat, Joey jumped and dropped his hoe or chopped out a potato instead of a weed. How could he put his mind on work when Dirk's next words might be, "Well, now, this seems a good time to go to the bank."

Anna watched anxiously as Joey poked at his midday meal. "Joey, what hurts? Is it your stomach? *Ach*, Dirk, the boy is not well! No appetite last night, and now this!"

"Anna, don't fuss so," Dirk grumbled. "It is the heat, nothing more." To Joey, he said, "Today no more gardening, *yah?* Go have a swim instead; that will bring back the appetite."

What a heaven-sent reprieve! That meant no trip to the bank today. And with every passing hour there was less chance that Anna would dip into the teapot for grocery money. Hope flickered in Joey's heart as he trotted off to the city pool. If he just lucked out till bedtime (he crossed his fingers), he'd have it made!

Still ahead of him, of course, was another scary midnight trip to the kitchen to return the ten-dollar bill and take a smaller one. But now that he'd done it once successfully, the thought wasn't quite so fearsome. Anyway, he'd be smarter this time. He'd make sure Pa's flashlight was where he could lay hands on it in the dark. Fingers couldn't tell the size of a bill; he needed eyes for that.

Some of the tension went out of Joey's taut shoulders as he sat on a park bench, watching children splash in the pool. Soon his only problem would be how to earn two dollars quickly, so he could put back the money he'd had to borrow.

"Shucks, nothin' to it!" Joey told himself confidently. Why, look, already this afternoon he'd made some of it—just by sitting here instead of going swimming! A swim cost fifteen cents if a kid didn't have a season ticket. So now he was only a dollar eighty-five short!

"Hey, that's a pretty neat way to make money!" thought Joey, his spirits perking up more and more. Ought to be lots of things—especially after school started next week—that he could say he needed and then do without.

Didn't sound quite honest, Joey admitted uncomfortably. But golly, it was his own money he was playing tricks with, wasn't it? If Pa weren't so nosy about how much he earned and what he did with every penny, Joey wouldn't be put to all this jugglery and—well, maybe cheating *was* the word.

Yes, it was Pa's fault, not his! Defiantly, on his homeward way, Joey stopped to dampen his hair and swim trunks in the spray of a lawn sprinkler. More tricks, more dishonesty, all made necessary by Pa's unreasonable attitude, he thought as he rounded the last corner.

A strange car was parked in their driveway, and a strange woman talking to Dirk. Anna stood on the porch, her hands rolled in her apron. The sight sent a tickly chill down Joey's spine. Always, when a family argument threatened, Anna rolled and unrolled her apron like that.

"Joey!" Dirk's voice was cold firm steel. The single word confirmed Joey's foreboding. Slowly, reluctantly, he went forward. "The lady has something to say to you."

"Yeh—yes, ma'am?" Joey stammered.

The stranger looked uneasy, as though wishing she could go away and pretend she'd never come. "I didn't want to make trouble—it's just that, well, it *is* a mess and—" She took a deep breath and finished firmly, "I want it cleaned up, that's all. A neighbor said the *Journal* carrier on our road sold fresh vegetables, so I called the *Journal* office for your name and address... Well, you *are* the boy who dumped the stuff in our pond, aren't you?"

Dirk broke the awful silence that followed. "Answer her, Joey!"

Dumbly, Joey could only nod.

Dirk said, "The boy will take care of it. Now."

"That's fine, then." The stranger looked unhappily from Dirk's stern face to Joey's low-hanging head. "I'm sorry if I've made trouble—"

"No trouble," said Dirk heavily. "I thank you, missus."

The lady backed her car out of the drive and darted away as though fleeing a stirred-up nest of hornets.

Dirk said, "Get the rake and a basket. You will show me where this pond is."

Silently Joey did as he was told. Silently, hands rolled even more tightly in her apron, Anna watched them get into the car. Silently they drove off, the awful black weight of quiet broken only by Joey's mumbled directions: "Turn right next corner," or "Go left here," and finally, "Stop."

There was the House. And there was the pond. At sight of it Joey wanted to dive in and never come up. Why had he thought water would hide the ruined vegetables? They'd floated to the top, of course. Straggles of cornsilk and green husk trailed out from almost pecked-clean cobs. Bunches of radishes bobbed just under the surface. Carrots wore slimy, soaked fronds of green.

Dirk studied the mess. Joey could practically hear the calculator in his brain clicking away as Dirk counted every vegetable and came up to a total that proved Joey had sold nothing yesterday. Not one single thing.

But when Dirk spoke, it was only to say, "Get to work."

Joey looked miserably up and down the road. By great good luck it was empty. But he knew that even if it were crowded with gawking, giggling spectators, he'd have to get out of the car and retrieve every last limp, drowned vegetable.

Head down, he plunged into the bushes. Thorny blackberry tendrils tore at his arms and T-shirt. The alarmed ducks set up a great quacking. Nervously Joey sneaked a look at the House. He half expected to see an entire family lined up—arms folded, faces grim, toes tapping—as they watched to see that he didn't miss so much as a radish.

There was no one in sight. The House seemed as empty as it had been all summer long. But Joey, red with exertion and embarrassment, was suspicious of its quiet; he was sure that condemning eyes watched him from every window.

"There he is!" the eyes said. "There's that awful boy who dumped garbage in our pond! *Tchk, tchk,* now he's frightened the ducks! Must he be so clumsy?"

Joey tried to hunch himself into half his size. He worked faster and faster. Water splashed in fountains; the ducks scolded loudly. Joey lunging for the last out-of-reach carrot, landed—*splosh!*—in their quacking midst.

Dripping water and lily pads, clutching the slimy carrot, Joey climbed out on the bank. His ear tips were scarlet. Carefully he averted his eyes from the accusing windows as he lugged the basket of rescued vegetables over to the car.

Dirk, who had stood rocklike on the bank this whole dreadful hour, moved now to lift the basket into the trunk.

Joey looked down at his soaked and streaming denims. "Maybe I better ride there too," he suggested. Dirk said nothing, so Joey hopped over the bumper and crouched cross-legged beside his oozing basket. Anything was better than sitting beside his silent father during the endless ride home. Wasn't Pa *ever* going to speak? Joey would rather have been yelled at, or even clobbered, than endure this awful silence.

As Dirk put the car in gear Joey glanced furtively back at the House. A car was just swinging into the driveway, the same car that not so long ago had appeared at Joey's house. Joey felt a smidgen of relief; maybe there hadn't been eyes at the windows after all. Maybe the House had been as empty as it had looked.

He scrunched lower in the trunk, trying to make himself invisible as they drove off down the road. A last peek at the House showed him what looked like an entire family spilling out of the car—big, little, middle-sized, two-legged, four-legged . . .

Even at this distance there was no mistaking the portly form just scrambling from the car—or the voice raised in loud *Ah-ooooooo!* as Texas Gay Bugler III, picked up the scent of strangers and high-tailed it toward the pond. "Him!" said Joey indignantly. So that's where the kid lived who'd caused all this trouble in the first place! He and his stupid dog! Wouldn't you just know that along with his fancy pooch he'd have a fancy home too?

Joey scowled and balled his fists. If fair was fair, the kid should've cleaned his own pond! Boy, Joey'd like to tell him a thing or two . . . and with his fists, *pow, splat, crunch!*

The fires of resentment warmed Joey till they arrived home. Then a glimpse of Dirk's face doused the glow. Anna was not in sight. Joey helped dump the vegetables on the compost pile, then muttered, "Gotta get my papers out," and shuffled toward the door.

Still not a word from Dirk. Whatever decision was forming in his mind, it was taking a long, long time to jell. And the longer it took—Joey brooded as he changed into clean shirt and suntans—the harder would be the final impact.

It was collection day on Joey's route. Joey didn't like asking for payment; it was almost as difficult as selling vegetables. But today he welcomed the excuse it gave him to stay away longer. He dawdled over each delivery; he was deliberate in making change; he called on every single customer, even the cranky ones whom he usually postponed to a later day—and a later day—sometimes managing to miss them entirely.

When at last he had to go home, the bulk of money in his pocket made it easier to pass Dirk, who sat on the back steps smoking his pipe.

Joey jingled coins loudly as he entered the kitchen. To his mother he boasted, "Sure hauled in the dough today! Every customer paid up."

"*Ach,* that's good!" Anna looked timidly at Dirk, standing in the doorway, then said no more. Once again silence closed around Joey, its weight squelching his brief attempt at bravado.

He went upstairs to put his money away, and was further subdued by sight of the bills he'd taken from the teapot. Here he'd gone to the scary trouble of borrowing that money—and all for nothing, now that Pa knew he hadn't sold a nickel's worth of stuff yesterday.

Joey folded the ten-dollar bill and the one together into a very small square and tucked it deep in his pants pocket. Maybe he'd have a chance, while Ma was busy with supper, to sneak them back into the teapot.

Anna, however, had supper on the table by the time he got downstairs.

Afterward Joey didn't have to be reminded of bedtime. He went extra early, taking off only his shoes and rolling fully dressed under the covers. Again he lay awake, waiting for the nighttime routine of Dirk's and Anna's retirement, giving them plenty of time to fall asleep.

At last all was quiet. Joey slipped out of bed. Noiselessly he opened his door and, avoiding the board that creaked, padded softly downstairs.

The flashlight came cool and ready to his hand. It led him to the kitchen . . . the counter . . . the cupboard door . . . the shelf with the teapot—

"Who's out there? What's going on?" The thundering roar froze Joey in dreadful immobility. *Click!* went the kitchen light, its white glare trapping Joey on the kitchen counter, one upraised paralyzed hand still reaching for the teapot.

6

○○○○○○○○○

NO NIGHTMARE WAS ever so dreadful.

"*Stealing!*" said Dirk.

"No—no, honest I wasn't!" Joey found his voice at last—if that high, strained squeak *was* his voice. "I wasn't stealing it; I was putting it back!"

Even to his own ears the words were damning. For why would he be putting money back into the teapot unless he had stolen it earlier? Despairingly Joey cried, "I *didn't* steal it! I didn't!"

Anna appeared behind Dirk in the kitchen doorway, a wrapper clutched around her, her gray hair in its nighttime braid. "What is it? What has happened?"

Dirk said heavily, "Our son is a thief."

"No!" cried Anna.

"No!" protested Joey. He flung the wadded bills away from him as though their touch burned his sweaty palm. "I'm not, I'm not! I only *borrowed* it." His parents' shocked, sorrowing faces told him they couldn't see the difference. Borrowing, stealing. One and the same.

When all seems lost, attack is sometimes the only

defense. So now Joey, his back to the wall, turned fiercely on Dirk.

"It's all your fault!" he shouted. The arguments assembled earlier in the day leaped ready to his tongue. "All your fault! Alla time havin' to know how much money I got—makin' me put it in the bank. Creeps, it's my money, isn't it? I guess I gotta right to do what I want with my own money!"

Dirk's answer came in words as heavy as paving stones. "It is not your money."

"Whaddya mean, it's not my money? I earned it, didn't I? I guess I gotta right—"

"You are a child. Until you are twenty-one your earnings belong to your parents."

Joey stared at his father, open-mouthed. "That's not *fair*—"

"I have been more than fair." Dirk spoke slowly, precisely, out of heavy sadness. "I could rightfully have used the money for your food and clothing. In my boyhood I did not even see my earnings; they were paid directly to my father."

Passionately Joey protested, "That's the *old* country! They don't do things that way here!"

"Law is law," said Dirk. "Come with me."

"*Ach*, Dirk—" Anna's distressed gaze followed Dirk as, one firm hand on Joey's shoulder, he led the sputtering, weeping, struggling boy upstairs.

41

To tell the truth (though Joey wouldn't have admitted it), his struggles were mostly a matter of principle. Joey knew he'd been asking for a licking from the moment he dumped the vegetables in the pond. Now it was here, and actually—though he yelled and kicked—it was a relief to get it over with. A licking cleared the air and washed the slate clean of his sins. A licking meant that his mounting tangle of problems, like an illness, had reached its crisis and would soon end.

Or so it had always been. Tonight was a different story. The whacking ended, Dirk said sternly. "It is plain you are not yet ready to deal with money. Money is a responsibility and a trust. Until you show yourself capable, I will take charge of your earnings."

"No!" yelled Joey. "You can't . . . they're mine . . . stop it, stop it, stop it!" His protests showered the air like confetti and with as little effect. In a frenzy of indignation he scratched and bit and pounded the unyielding hands that opened his dresser drawer and took out his money jar and savings-account book. "Thief!" croaked Joey like a furious bluejay. "Thief! Thief! *You're* the thief!"

Undeterred, Dirk moved him aside and left the room. The door clicked firmly shut behind him. Joey kicked it in helpless fury. "Just you wait!" he raged, hiccoughing on angry sobs. "You'll be sorry!"

It was awful to be treated like this! Outrage dried Joey's tears and colored his memory of the events leading up to Dirk's action. Now when he recalled the scene in the kitchen—the scared boy trapped on the counter, Anna's grocery money in his hand—it was with indignation. Creeps, what was so terrible about a couple of bills spending the night in his money jar instead of the teapot? He was putting them back, wasn't he? All he'd needed was one little minute to explain!

But did he get it? Huh, fat chance! Right away Pa had to jump all over him . . . call him a thief . . . take his own money away from him—

What he ought to do was run away. Yeh, that'd shake 'em up! He could hike across town to the freeway, hitch a ride, maybe be clear out of the state by morning. On his way back to Iowa and the farm and . . .

How long would it take him? Depended on how lucky he was getting rides. Maybe four, five days. He could make out that long on hamburgers and milk—

Bought with what? He hadn't a single solitary cent—*wouldn't* have till next month's *Journal* collections.

Or would Pa be waiting to grab them too?

Frustrated, Joey flung himself on the bed and thumped it with both fists. Every way he turned he

came up against a dead end. And what was he supposed to do about school, for Pete's sake? Ask Pa
every time he needed a dime for notebook paper? *Ask
him for his own money?* Joey whammed a pillow
against the headboard. Like heck he would! He'd use
grocery sacks and wrapping paper!

Long before morning Joey's rage gave way to sullen despair. All his ideas for revenge were spent, and
he was left staring dry-eyed at the starlit sky beyond
his window, like a prisoner looking through bars.

Sleep crept up on him. He rolled over and
buried his face in his crossed arms. His last waking
thought was a tight-lipped promise: Never, no, never
would he ask Dirk for a penny of his own money! Nor
would he earn another nickel as long as it had to go
into Dirk's keeping.

II

ooooooooo

The Coming
of Eric

7

○○○○○○○○○

AFTER THE QUARREL, home to Joey became an enemy camp where he was temporarily held captive.

Dirk gave orders; Joey obeyed them—just barely. Dirk continued to load the red wagon each afternoon; Joey brought it back at dusk, untouched. In the garden two weeds grew for every one he pulled. In the house his chores were done so slowly and badly, they only just missed not being done at all.

True to his promise, Joey didn't ask for money, even on the first day of school—though what he'd do without it, he didn't know. Books were furnished free, but what about all the other expenses? Well, no matter; he wasn't asking Pa for a handout from his own savings, no, sir!

Anna fussed over him as he ate his cereal and toast. "Did you polish your shoes, Joey? Are your fingernails clean? Let me see once."

"Aw, gee, Ma, you'd think I was a kindergartner!"

"*Na, na,* I know. Seventh grade, already. Do you have your report card, Joey, so they know where you belong?"

47

"They'll find out," Joey mumbled. It was one of his biggest worries that he'd be found wanting in some requirement and shamefully put back a grade.

"Ah, well," Anna sighed, "I go get your lunch sack so you don't forget it."

Dirk came in as Joey finished his second helping of oatmeal. Joey concentrated on chasing the last pearly gray fleck around the bottom of his bowl. With slow deliberation, Dirk counted out seven dollar-bills and laid them at Joey's plate.

"So now, you buy what you need," he said.

Joey looked at the bills with loathing. Big deal! His own money, doled out like charity or something! He'd like to leave it lying right there, just walk out of the room without touching it!

But the hard truth was, he did have to have it. Well, there was victory in the fact that he *hadn't* asked for it . . . and Pa knew he wouldn't.

Hopkins Junior High presented a different battleground. Joey approached it cautiously. Face impassive, eyes showing just a slit of blue beneath hooded lids, he watched, then very casually imitated the other boys who straggled toward the main entrance.

Bike in rack, so. Give it a final kick to test its steadiness. Stroll toward the door, hands in pockets. (Nobody else was carrying a lunch sack, so Joey left his in the bike basket.)

Inside Hopkins, the picture was more confused. Registration desks were set up in the halls. Students milled around and called greetings to their friends. A gray-haired lady—a teacher, maybe?—circulated among them, saying, "All right now, get in line. If you don't know where you belong, just ask me."

Joey didn't know, but he wasn't about to confess his ignorance. He chose a line at random and shuffled along with it while he got his bearings. The desk he was approaching (he peeked around the tall girl ahead of him) bore a card, printed "M-Z" . . . well, that ought to be the place for Van Oolbekink.

Not until he was almost at the desk did he peek again and see another card with the number "8."

Eighth grade? "Ulp!" said Joey and bolted out of line.

The gray-haired lady appeared immediately. "Need some help? What's your name and grade?"

"Seventh," Joey muttered, just barely audible. "Van Oolbekink."

"I didn't quite hear—did you say Oobelking?"

"Kink!" Joey's voice broke and the word came out in a loud squeak. A giggle rippled down the line like wind over meadow grass. Crimson with embarrassment Joey rumbled, "Joey Van Oolbekink, seventh grade."

The gray-haired lady quelled the giggle with a

frown. "Of course," she said, as though the name
turned up on her rolls as often as Smith or Jones.
"Well, Joey, you go on up to the next corner and
turn— Wait a minute!" Her searching gaze selected a
boy just passing them. "Here's someone who'll help
you—Bob! Bob Barton!"

"Hi, Mrs. Meade."

At the sound of the voice Joey's heart went *plunk*,
then set up a muffled drumming in his ears. He turned,
glowering, to face the boy from the House, owner of
the upsetting beagle.

"Bob, this is Joey Van Oolbekink. He's new
here. Will you help him register? . . . Bob's a seventh-
grader too," she explained to Joey, "but he's visited
us so often, he can answer all your questions."

"Sure, Mrs. Meade," said Bob. "Come on, Joey."
He gave the scowling boy a second glance. "Hey, I
know you! You're the kid—"

"Yeh," Joey growled. "Skip it! I don't need any
help." He plunged through the eighth-grade line to
escape more quickly.

"Hey, watch it!" a boy protested.

"*You* watch it," his friend laughed. "Didn't you
hear? He's the Kink!"

"Yeh, that's right—take it easy, Kink!"

A girl giggled. Laughter followed Joey till he
rounded the corner. Bob, close by him, panted, "Hey,

50

what's the hurry? Here's your line."

"C'n see it myself," muttered Joey, red-eared from the laughter. "Think I'm blind or somethin'?"

"Well, okay! So why do you rate a guide?" Joey's surliness had ruffled Bob's temper. " 'Cause you *are* the Kink?"

Joey spun around, fists balled, chin jutted forward. "You better not say that again!"

"Yeh? Why not?"

" 'Cause you'll get a poke in the puss, that's why not!"

"Oh, yeh? Jus' like to see you try it!"

Joey scowled ferociously. "You'll see, all right!"

"Then you better have your bodyguard handy to pick up the pieces—Kink!"

Joey swung—a wild punch that Bob countered with outthrust elbow. Momentum carried Joey forward; the elbow connected with his nose. Blood spurted. A girl squealed; a boy yelled, "Yeow—fight!" Joey lowered his head and rammed Bob below the ribs.

"Oof!" Bob was staggered, but only for a moment. Fists cocked, jaw tucked in, he charged.

"Boys! Boys!" Mrs. Meade came hurrying around the corner. The principal popped out of his office. "What's the meaning of this?" Stern hands separated the battlers.

51

Mrs. Meade looked sorrowfully from Bob's doubled fists to Joey's streaming nose. "Bob, what a thing to do! When I asked you to look after Joey!"

Joey was stung. "Don't need lookin' after!"

"Naw, he's a big shot!" And Bob added, just under his breath, "He's the Kink!"

Joey, struggling against the restraining hands, aimed a kick at Bob's shins. Bob kicked back. The principal said, "All right, you two! Stop your scuffling or you can spend the day in my office!"

Scowling and muttering something that sounded like "A day with the Kink? Yipes!", Bob went off down the hall. Joey glared after him; his chest swelled till he almost couldn't breathe. Every time Bob Barton entered his life, his pride was whittled into sawdust curls. From head to toe Joey ached with a mutinous need to show the whole student body of Hopkins Junior High (but especially Bob Barton) that Joey Van Oolbekink was Somebody.

Mrs. Meade brought him a handkerchief dampened in cold water. "I just don't understand it," she murmured.

Joey did. It was exactly what he expected of school in Westport. Trouble. Everybody against him, the outlander who didn't belong here. When at noon, properly registered at last, he went out to get his lunch sack and found the bicycle basket empty, he wasn't really surprised. It fitted the picture.

Sulky, miserable, lonely, his stomach growling with hunger, Joey spent lunch hour in a solitary corner of Hopkins, feeling sorry for himself.

8

ooooooooo

REGISTRATION DAY was bad. The weeks following were worse.

To begin with, Joey's name made trouble for him. Teachers stumbled over it; his classmates thought it funny. And that detested nickname, given him the first day, kept sprouting up like a weed whose roots stretch all the way to China!

Joey was angry and resentful. What was so funny about Van Oolbekink? Back home it had been just another Dutch name in a town of Dutch names. Like Vanderpohlen and Frieslander and Mastbergen and Kleinhesselink.

But in Westport the names were English: Johnson, Harris, Smith, Barton. Easy to spell, easy to pronounce. In Westport, Van Oolbekink was an alien name that triggered so many scraps it sometimes looked as if Joey would spend his entire seventh grade in the principal's office.

Most of the scraps were with Bob. It seemed that whenever the two boys met—*ssszzz! sssttt!*—the air was filled with smoke and fire and instant bloodshed.

"I didn't start it!" Bob would protest as once

again the boys were hauled to the principal's office.

"Wasn't me," mumbled Joey, glowering at the bigger boy.

"Then how *did* it start?" the principal demanded.

Neither boy could say. To tell the truth, they didn't really know. All it needed was a word, a look, a jostle and *szzzzzzzz!*—there were those sparks again!

What Joey's simmering discontent boiled down to was the need to prove that anything Bob Barton could do, Joey could do—better.

Bob went out for football. Very promptly Joey went out for football.

"Ought to have more heft for this game," the coach told him dubiously. "A kid your size could get tromped to jelly."

"I'm real tough," Joey assured him, doubling his arm to show his muscle, "and too fast to get tromped!"

The coach was not convinced. "Seems to me you'd do better in track. Might make a pretty good sprinter."

"I don't *want* to run!" Joey protested. Compared to a hulking helmeted football player, a trackman in his skimpy shorts and singlet would look like a sissy. "I want to play *football!*"

"Well, we'll give it a try," the coach said.

So far, Joey had spent most of practice time on

the bench—resentfully watching Bob shape up into the rookie team's best center.

Bob played clarinet in beginners' band. Joey promptly elected to play drums. Drums (as well as being furnished by the school) made more noise than a clarinet. Under Joey's thrashing attack they made a great deal more noise.

Again and again the band director stopped him. "Joey, that's not the way to hold your sticks. Shake hands with the left one—gently, gently—and let the other balance on your right hand, so! Now tap the beat *lightly*—don't rush it—"

Wham-slam-bang-crunch went Joey's sticks, faster and faster, louder and louder. *Wham! Slam! Bang! Crunch! WHAMSLAMBANGCRUNCH!* Nobody was going to hear the clarinet section if *he* could help it!

Bob chose as his activity 4-H. So did Joey. Both had been 4-H members for years. Bob was a rock hound; he collected and sorted and polished stones. Joey's specialty had been livestock, but he couldn't raise a heifer or even a goat on Orchard Lane—not next door to Mrs. Wickshire.

"How about putting in a garden?" Mr. Sanford, the 4-H director, suggested. "Winters are so mild here, you can plant any time."

"No!" Joey rejected the idea violently. As yet he

hadn't chosen a project, but he'd come up with something (he promised himself) that'd make Bob's bunch of rocks look about as important as a kid's tiddlywinks. Yessir, anything Bob Barton could do, Joey could do—better! *Anything*.

Then in late September the Westport Kennel Club held its annual dog-show. Disbelieving, roiled with envy, Joey saw the pictures of the prize winners in the Sunday paper—"Texas Gay Bugler III, Best of Breed"—and Bob holding the ribbon, grinning like Christmas morning.

"That ol' mutt?" fumed Joey. "Musta been th' only beagle in the show!" Burning with resentment, he dropped the paper on the floor and tromped over it. Why should some kids have *everything?* It wasn't fair.

Bob brought the ribbon with him to school Monday, and Mrs. Meade made the dog-show the current-events topic for Social Living class.

"Tell us all about it," she invited Bob. "We'd like to know how an owner shows his dog and on what points a dog is judged—wouldn't we, class?"

While Bob happily made his report Joey sat in sizzling silence. Wasn't the guy *ever* going to shut up? On and on and on he went about his stupid dog and the stupid show, all the time waving that stupid ribbon like a decoration from the President of the

United States. Boy, did he think *he* was something!

Afterward, during class break, Joey managed to bump Bob in the crowded hall. "Hey, who ya shovin'?" yelped Joey, and unleashed such a wild-swinging punch that he missed his target entirely—

And hit a towering ninth grader!

If the big boy had socked him in return, Joey wouldn't have been half so hurt as by what actually happened. For the ninth grader scooped Joey up like a disobedient puppy and held him—kicking and struggling—at arm's length.

"Well, if it isn't the Kink!" he said, laughing.

"Lemme down!" Joey bellowed. His flailing fists and kicking feet landed short of his big tormentor. "LEMME DOWN!"

The bell sounded for the next class. "Sure thing, Kink," said the big boy cheerfully and dropped him with a thump. Joey was left sputtering and sizzling, knuckling the angry tears that filled his eyes.

He *wouldn't* go back to class! Everyone would snicker. Darn ol' Bob, it was all his fault—shovin' a guy and then not being there when you hit him!

The hall emptied quickly. Joey, still muttering to himself, scuffled along one side. Every few steps he kicked a locker door or twirled its combination lock. If the racket brought the principal from his office or a teacher from her classroom, that was all right with

Joey. He was spoiling for a fight and he didn't much care who provided it.

Nobody appeared, though. The last classroom door closed; the hall was now totally Joey's. Frustrated, he gave the next locker door an extra-strong kick . . .

And it swung open. In the moment before he slammed it shut, Joey saw a jacket and books—

And a scattering of coins, half hidden under a baseball mitt.

9

○○○○○○○○○

MONEY, OR THE lack of it, had become Joey's greatest problem. The bills given him on registration day had been promptly spent on locker deposits and school supplies. Then the very next week Mrs. Meade instructed her Social Living class to buy English workbooks. How was Joey to get fifty cents for a workbook without asking Dirk?

Further complications came quickly. The science teacher planned a field trip—a whole day up in the black lava country. Each student was to contribute a quarter toward the day's expenses.

Mr. Sanford reminded them to pay their 4-H dues . . .

The band was taking up a collection for a picnic on Band Day . . .

And notebook paper disappeared at alarming speed. *What* was he to do?

His paper route was gone. After the humiliating scene at the duck pond, Joey wouldn't go near that area till after dark. His customers there waited with increasing impatience for their papers. More and more of them telephoned the *Journal* office: "What's the matter? Where's my *Journal?*"

"What's going on, Joey?" the *Journal* manager asked. "You were one of my best boys. Now shape up—I don't want to hear any more complaints."

But he did. So at last there was nothing for him to do but take Joey off the route. Now he needn't make another monthly collection only to surrender it to Dirk.

But without the paper route, he had no income at all. Dirk, growly as a bear over the loss of the route and Joey's stubborn do-nothing attitude at home, hadn't given him another dime. Nor would Joey ask for it. So there the two of them were—at a stalemate. Joey didn't guess how perplexed and troubled Dirk was; he only knew that his own situation was getting critical.

So far, he had stalled paying dues; he had avoided collections; he had postponed buying his English workbook (though he was getting dangerously behind on the exercises). When he ran out of notebook paper, he quit turning in assignments. But that was a deadend with no turning space.

"Joey," Mrs. Meade had reminded him just this morning, "your book report is overdue."

"Yes'm," admitted Joey.

"Well, get it in by Friday, or I'll have to give you

61

an F. And your English grade can't stand any more F"s. Joey, what's happened to you? You started out so well."

Joey had no answer. Nor had he any prospect of avoiding the F—until the door of locker 121 swung open. Though he had promptly slammed it shut and continued down the hall, the picture of the coins on the shelf was burned on his inner eye. How much had there been?

"Wouldn't hurt any to count it," Joey told himself defensively. Just to see how much a stupid kid like that would leave in an unlocked locker. Some rich kid, probably, got a big allowance, and when it was gone just asked for more. Bet *his* father never grabbed his earnings!

Without realizing he was doing so, Joey had gone back to locker 121. Now his hand went out to pull open the door and shove aside the mitt. A quarter, three dimes, a nickel, four pennies . . . sixty-four cents. Enough for notebook paper and the workbook.

"No," said his brain, waking up and trying to take charge, "don't do it. No, no, no, no . . ."

But his fingers moved of their own accord, as if they belonged to someone else, and the coins slid into his pocket.

Joey's heart beat so loudly it muffled the hum from the classrooms. In a sudden, not-to-be-explained gust of anger, he kicked the locker door hard before charging down the hall.

"All his fault!" he stormed. "All his fault!"

But whether he meant the boy who had left the coins unguarded . . . or Bob Barton, who was the cause of Joey's being in the hall instead of in class . . . or Dirk, who by depriving him of his own money had made theft necessary—Joey didn't know.

10

ALL THAT DAY the money remained in Joey's pocket—its faint jingle as ominous as a bell tolling.

He waited fearfully for an outcry about stolen money. Each time the intercom crackled in a classroom, Joey flinched. But the words issuing from the little box said nothing about a theft.

Maybe the boy hadn't reported his loss. Maybe he'd even forgotten having the money in his locker! Slowly, muscle by aching muscle, Joey relaxed. Fear gave way to relief, and relief to confidence. He'd gotten away with it.

When, the next day, there was still no uproar about the money, Joey could even jingle the coins as he went to his classes, enjoying their jaunty music.

"Joey," said the science teacher, "don't forget to bring your quarter for the field trip."

"Got it right here," said Joey—and plunked down a quarter like a millionaire.

"Joey," said the girl passing the collection box in band, "do you want to put something in toward the picnic?"

"Oh, sure," said Joey—and tossed a dime into the box with lordly ease.

"Class," said Mrs. Meade, "I want all workbooks turned in this Friday with the first four exercises completed."

"Ulp," said Joey. He'd forgotten to save enough money for the workbook. And there were 4-H dues. Once again hopelessness settled on him like a dark and very heavy cloud.

He didn't want to steal; he had no intention of stealing ever again. But now in spite of himself he began sneaking sidelong glances at every locker he passed.

Of course an open locker was no guarantee of money inside. But if there just *happened* to be some lying around, and if Joey just *happened* to be alone in the hall . . .

"It isn't stealing!" Joey reassured himself. "I'll put every penny back, soon as I get my money from Pa." To prove his sincerity, he had made a tiny, cryptic entry in the back of his notebook: "121—64¢."

By midweek another notation appeared beneath the first in his notebook: "154—15¢." And then another: "239—10¢."

And still the intercom was mute about his crimes. Joey was less scared now when the box on the wall crackled; his forays into the halls grew more daring.

On Friday, still far short of the total he needed, Joey spotted the gaping crack of an unlocked locker on his way to Social Living class. Locker 297, Joey noted quickly.

Ten minutes after class started, his hand was waving in the air. "C'n I be excused?"

Mrs. Meade looked at him and sighed. This week Joey seemed always in need of being excused.

"All right. But get back promptly; you're missing too much class time."

Joey ducked out of the room. The hall was empty except for the girl from the principal's office collecting attendance slips at the classroom doors. Joey dawdled over the drinking fountain till she rounded the corner. Then he walked purposefully down the hall toward the boys' washroom—past locker 297—pivoted swiftly, and opened the locker door. Wedged between a stack of books and a bulky sweater was a girl's purse. A purse! Golly, he couldn't stand here in the hall fumbling through a purse—

In one quick motion, Joey had it out of the locker and under his jacket. Not until he was safely behind the bolted door of a toilet stall did he open his prize. What a jumble! Pink curlers, wads of Kleenex, comb, scribbled paper, bobby pins . . .

And in the zippered pocket a roll of bills. No coins, just a folded and refolded wad of bills.

Joey was scared. Goose pimples came up on his arms. This was Money! Anyone losing a chunk like this would blow the roof off old Hopkins!

"Chee—I better get it back in that locker *pronto!*"

Shivers chased each other down his back at the thought of walking through the hall with all this loot. Should he just leave it here and hightail back to class?

Wait a minute. . . . What if the next boy to come in here made off with the money? The dragnet would be out for anyone who'd been excused from class this morning. They'd pick him up and grill him—Joey's imagination etched the vivid scene at the police station—till he confessed to taking the purse. Then who'd believe he hadn't stolen the money?

Joey summoned up all his nerve, thrust the flattened purse beneath his jacket where his elbow could hold it securely, and left the washroom.

Locker 297. There it was, almost at the head of the stairs. Only a few steps more. The hall was empty of witnesses . . .

"Boy, you sure take your time!"

11

○○○○○○○○○

JOEY NEARLY DROPPED the purse from under his arm. He jerked around to see Bob Barton coming up the stairs, loaded chin-high with rolls of paper.

"Here I been all the way to the library 'n' back, gettin' these posters for Mrs. Meade, an' you're still goofin' off! Here, grab some, they're slippin'."

"Grab 'em yourself," Joey retorted shakily. If he moved his arm, the purse would surely slip. "You're the one tryin' to butter up the teacher!"

"Yeh?" Bob flared.

"Yeh!" Joey moved rapidly down the hall toward the Social Living classroom. Bob looked ready to drop the posters and come in slugging, and Joey was in no position right now to fight. He loped into the classroom just three paces ahead of Bob and dived for his seat.

The purse bulged against his ribs, big as an albatross and equally unshakable. How was he to get rid of it? Mrs. Meade wouldn't excuse him twice in the same hour. But if he waited till class break, the hall would be swarming with kids. The girl might go to her locker . . .

Joey's stomach churned; his face paled to a greenish-white. His arm was already growing numb from cramping it so tensely against his side. Could he sneak the thing into his desk? Why was everyone staring at him?

"Joey!" It was the second time Mrs. Meade had called his name. "Will you come to the board and—"

Joey shook his head. "Dunno!"

"You don't even know what I was going to ask you to do!"

"Dunno anyway!" Panic stiffened Joey's resistance. To stand with his back to the class, every movement of his writing arm pulling his jacket tighter across that dreadful bulge—no, he didn't dare.

But how long could he hold out, even just sitting here quietly? If his arm went to sleep, he might let the purse slip and not even know it! Gingerly he flexed his arm muscles and winced at the waking-up prickles.

Mrs. Meade glanced at him curiously, then with concern. The boy's color wasn't good—and he was holding his arm peculiarly, as though he'd hurt it! He and Bob Barton had returned to the room at almost the same moment, both looking furious. . . .

"Joey, is something wrong with your arm?"

"Huh? N-no!" Terrified, Joey squeezed his arm closer to his side; his face grew even more pale.

Mrs. Meade was convinced her suspicion was correct. Yes, the boys had been roughhousing in the hall; a push, a stumble, a fall—goodness knows it didn't take much of an accident to break a bone! She scribbled on a pad and tore off the top sheet.

"Better have the nurse take a look at it, Joey, just to be sure. Here, take this permit to her office."

Joey almost keeled over. Relief sent the blood surging so rapidly to his head, he staggered dizzily as he got to his feet.

Anxiously Mrs. Meade asked, "Do you want someone to go with you?"

"*No!*" Joey gulped. He almost snatched the miraculous permit from her hand as he plunged past her to the door.

Outside in the blessedly empty hall, he lurched for locker 297 like a spent swimmer exerting his last ounce of strength to reach shore, shoved the dreadful purse back on the locker shelf, slammed the door, and spun the lock.

There! It was done. He was safe—but so weak that his knees buckled. He stumbled downstairs to another washroom (he didn't think he would *ever* use the one on second floor again!) and sloshed his face with cold water. Boy, that felt good! Boy, it was great to use both arms again! Boy, he was sure of one thing: he was never, *never* going to open another locker than his own, ever again. *Boy!*

Something silvery lay on the edge of the basin by the towel rack. With his eyes cleared of water, Joey saw it was a wristwatch. "Better turn it in to Lost and Found," thought Joey, and dropped it into his pocket.

Back once more in Social Living, Joey collapsed into his seat, weak way down to his toes.

Mrs. Meade noticed that he could now move both arms freely. "Did the nurse find anything wrong, Joey?"

"The nur—oh—uh, no'm. Nothin' much."

"That's good. Well, get out paper and pencil; we're going to have a spelling test."

Spelling was usually Joey's best subject. Not today, though! Mrs. Meade, entering the grades in her grade book after class, was startled to see check marks like red gashes after "decieved" and "aply" and "canery." Three mistakes on a spelling test of Joey's? Why, it was unthinkable! Was his arm hurting more than he'd let on?

In the cafeteria at lunchtime, joining the school nurse at a table, Mrs. Meade asked, "Well, what did Joey come up with this morning? At least you didn't send him back in splints."

"Joey?" asked the nurse.

"The Van Oolbekink boy. Fighting again, I'm afraid. How badly was his arm hurt?"

71

The nurse looked puzzled. "I don't know. I didn't see it."

"But I sent him to you first period . . ."

"He must have found a cure on the way," the nurse said cheerfully. "Too bad. I could use some first-aid practice! I've had nothing all week but little girls with big headaches."

Mrs. Meade, more puzzled than before, poked absent-mindedly at her spaghetti. Something was certainly wrong somewhere, and as Joey's homeroom teacher it was up to her to straighten it out. There was the way his schoolwork had fallen off after such a good start—his parents weren't going to be happy with his first report card from Hopkins . . .

"I wonder if I shouldn't have a talk with them?" she thought.

The strength returned to Joey's legs, but it was quite a while before his brain shifted out of low gear. He walked past the principal's office four times during the day without recollecting that the Lost and Found box was just inside the door. All he could think about was what a close call he'd had. That wad of money—how much had there been, anyway? Enough to put him in jail for *years*, probably, if he'd been caught with it! *Wowie!*

When Joey got home that afternoon, the watch was still in his pocket.

12

○○○○○○○○○

JOEY WAS TROUBLED to find he'd carried the watch away from school. He told himself, "I'll take it to Lost and Found first thing Monday morning."

A weekend was a long time to remember something, though. When Joey got to school Monday, he realized that the watch was still in his dresser drawer. "Oh, well, I'll bring it tomorrow," he told himself.

Then the classroom intercom crackled and the principal's voice said, "May I have your attention, please? A valuable watch has disappeared . . ."

Joey stared, appalled, at the little black box. All last week when he'd winced at its every sputter, it hadn't said a word about his thefts. Now, when he hadn't done anything but forget, it was after him!

The principal's voice went on with the announcement: If the finder of the watch would leave it in the Lost and Found box today, no questions would be asked.

Joey passed the box a dozen times during the day. Each time he carefully looked the other way. It wasn't his fault, he told the inner Joey, that he'd left the stupid watch at home; he hadn't *intended* to.

That night in his bedroom Joey examined the watch curiously. The case was thin and silvery, the band expandable, the face very plain, with clear, easy-to-read numbers and a sweep second hand. "Valuable," the principal had described it. How much did that mean it was worth?

And how did you get money from a watch anyway? In the movies the finder might take it to a pawnshop. Joey wasn't sure there even *was* a pawnshop in Westport—

Joey's thoughts jerked to a startled halt. What did he care about pawnshops? He was dropping this into the Lost and Found box first thing in the morning. Only reason he'd looked at it was to see what made a watch "valuable."

With his penknife he carefully pried open the case. Surely a lot of sparkle in there; must be seventeen or more tiny jewels in the works. On the inner side of the case was engraved some fine graceful script. Joey held the watch under his bedlight to read it.

"Bob from Mom and Dad" with a date underneath, Christmas a year ago. Bob.

Clear as a strip of film, Joey could see Bob Barton below him on the band risers, his raised hands holding the clarinet in air—and on his left wrist a thin silvery circle.

Sure, it'd be Bob's—wouldn't you know it? Darn thing was probably platinum or plutonium or something! Huh, what difference if Bob Barton lost a watch? His folks'd just buy him another.

Still and all, Joey supposed he'd have to return it. But it wouldn't hurt to let Bob stew over its loss awhile—might make him more careful next time!

On Wednesday (with the watch still in his dresser drawer) Joey saw a notice on the bulletin board:

REWARD! $15 for return of watch left in boys' washroom Friday. Finder may bring watch to Barton's Department Store and collect reward from cashier. *No questions asked.*

Fifteen dollars! Golly, Joey hadn't thought a watch cost more than that! Fifteen dollars—enough to solve his money problems for weeks and weeks and *weeks.*

All day the notice churned up excitement inside him. Did he dare try to collect the reward? Barton's was the biggest store in Westport; who'd notice one boy at a busy hour? "No questions asked," the notice had said. He could just shove the watch over the cashier's counter and she'd hand him the cash.

But what if Mr. Barton had a spy waiting

75

around? What if the cashier tipped the spy off with a wink or a nod, and he followed Joey out of the store . . .

Joey broke into heavy perspiration. He wiped his face and hands. Fifteen dollars—golly!

At home that night he slipped the watch deep into his jacket pocket so he'd be sure not to forget it the next day. Over and over as he tossed sleeplessly on his rumpled bed he rehearsed a speech.

"Friend of mine gimme this . . . said to bring it here and you'd pay a reward."

Then if someone did follow him, he'd have an out—he was only doing it for a friend. No, he couldn't name the friend; he was no welsher.

After school the following afternoon Joey skipped football practice and went downtown. Acting the part of an old pro at this game, cleverly laying a false trail, he wandered in and out of several stores on his way to Barton's. He lingered over counters, picked up items, and frowned at the price tags.

Next to Barton's was the five-and-dime, the last stop he could make. More and more deliberately Joey studied the merchandise on the counters to postpone the awful instant of entering Barton's store.

"Something for you?" a salesgirl asked.

"No—uh, jus' lookin'!" Joey stammered. In his

confusion he dropped the ball-point pen he was holding, dived for it, knocked others from the counter.
"Sorry"—red-faced, perspiring again, Joey groped
along the floor retrieving pens—"here y'are!"

Why was the salesgirl looking at him like that—
almost as though she could guess what weighted down
his jacket pocket! Panic assailed him. Stumbling,
bumping counters and caroming off customers, Joey
ran out of the store.

The fresh rain-misted air smacked his hot face
and slowed his racing pulse. Gratefully he took a deep
breath of it—

And then felt a hand on his shoulder. A stern
voice said, "Just a minute, son. Let's have the pens
you put in your pocket!"

Appalled, Joey turned to face the floorwalker
from the five-and-dime. "Whaddya mean? I don't
know what you're talkin' about—" His voice
squeaked; even to his own ears he sounded guilty. "I
didn't take nothin'—lemme go!"

The firm hand did nothing of the kind. Another
man came from the store to join them. The floor-
walker said, "I think we've caught one of that gang of
shoplifting kids, Mr. Matthews. I watched him quite
a few minutes. He didn't buy anything, just handled
considerable merchandise and then pulled the old

trick of dropping some on the floor."

"You're crazy—it was an accident—I put 'em all back!" Joey shrilled.

The manager said, "In that case you won't mind turning out your pockets, will you?"

"I don't have to! You can't make me!"

"Mr. Randall," said the manager, "would you just step down to the corner and ask Officer Doran to come here a minute? Much better to have this handled officially."

"Okay, okay!" yelled Joey. "See for yourself!" Frantically he dumped the oddments from his pockets —pencil stubs, crumpled paper, a bent nail, a button, paperclips, penknife . . .

With his hand in his jacket pocket, Joey froze. "Tha's all," he muttered.

"What's in that pocket? You're holding something in your hand—"

"Nothin'—nothin' at all!"

"Let me see it!" said the manager. The two men closed in on him like thunderclouds blotting out the sky.

Joey let out a frightened yelp. He lowered his head and like a bull-calf drove straight into the floor-walker's stomach.

"Oooof!" gasped the man. He released Joey to clasp his pained middle.

Past him Joey charged, zigzagging down the street, darting around pedestrians. Somebody shouted, "Stop him!" Hands reached out to grab—

Too late. Luck routed him across the street just as the light changed and traffic cut off pursuit. He was off and running!

13

DIRK WAS CLOSE to admitting defeat. On the day of the two phone calls, he told Anna, "We will go back to the farm. To come here was a mistake."

The day had been gloomy from the beginning. Fall rains had set in—hardly more than a mist, but constant. For a week they had scarcely seen the sun. To wake up to another dark day, when their hearts were already so shadowed, seemed almost too much to take.

But steadily, exchanging few words, Dirk and Anna had gone about their day's duties. While Anna tidied the house, Dirk shoveled a load of sawdust down the basement chute for the furnace—an odd sort of firewood, he thought wonderingly, but much used out here and costing little.

He had come into the kitchen for a cup of coffee and a brief spell of drying out, when the phone rang the first time.

It was Mrs. Meade.

"Mr. Van Oolbekink," she said hesitantly, "I feel we should have a conference about Joey."

"What has he done now?"

"It isn't so much what he's doing as what he isn't doing. His assignments are turned in late—or not at all. His grades aren't going to please you when you see his report card, and I don't understand it—he started off well. I've tried to talk to him about it, but he's so closed in, we simply don't make contact. I thought perhaps—well, if there were any trouble at home that I don't know about . . . "

Dirk said heavily, "There is no trouble."

"Oh, I see. Still—perhaps if you could come here for a talk, we might discover a clue to what's wrong . . ."

"I will talk to him."

"That isn't quite what I meant—"

"Good-bye."

To Anna he explained, "Joey's teacher. Some nonsense about a conference to find out why his grades are poor."

Anna asked, "You will talk to her?"

"It is pure foolishness. Either the boy is stupid and cannot do the work or he is lazy and will not, that's what it comes down to. If he is stupid, talk will not make him smarter. If he is lazy, then he must be made to work, and that takes more than words." Dirk gave a great sigh. "So there is no need for talk."

Anna looked as if she would like to answer. But

81

she had never argued with Dirk's decisions, and now she didn't know how to begin.

Four o'clock came. Four-thirty. Joey should be home from school. Five. Five-thirty.

Dirk's face was darker than the lowering sky. More and more often he appeared in the kitchen to check his pocketwatch by Anna's wall clock.

Then the phone rang for the second time. Again Dirk picked up the receiver.

"Mr. Van Oolbekink?" It was a man's voice this time. "This is Ralph Matthews at Holloway's Five-and-Dime. I'm afraid we have a problem on our hands, Mr. Van Oolbekink; frankly, I'm asking you to be very broad-minded and understanding. It may be we were unjust in accusing your son of shoplifting this afternoon—"

"What!" roared Dirk.

"Uh, well, to be brief, your son's actions struck our floorwalker as suspicious. We've had our troubles lately with a gang of schoolboys who have been shoplifting, so Mr. Randall may have been too ready to think the worst—"

"Say what you have to say!" Dirk thundered.

"Uh, yes," Mr. Matthews hurried on. "Well, to be brief, we asked him to show us the contents of his pockets. You must understand, Mr. Van Oolbekink, that we have been sadly victimized lately by a crowd of boys no older than your son. It was only natural that we should think—"

"Go on!"

"Yes, of course. Well, as I was saying, he emptied his pockets—*most* of his pockets—then took to his heels. That made us positive of his guilt till we checked the stock and—well, frankly, there doesn't seem to be anything missing. Whatever he had that he didn't want us to see—well, I have no basis for belief that it came from *our* store. His name was on one of the items—a piece of paper—he took from his pockets; that's how we were able to get in touch with you. We'll send you the items, and—well, to be brief, I certainly hope you understand our position, Mr. Van Oolbekink, and will harbor no hard feeling. . . ."

"Yes," said Dirk and hung up, leaving Mr. Matthews to wipe his perspiring face and wonder which question Dirk's monosyllable answered.

The anxiety in Anna's eyes was acute. Dirk reluctantly explained the phone call. "So that is where he has been," he finished. "Hanging around town. The sure way to get into trouble—if he isn't already."

"But where is he now?" Anna pleaded.

"Who knows?" Dirk pulled a chair out from the kitchen table. "We will eat before the food spoils entirely," he directed.

Two tears ran down Anna's cheeks as she filled

83

Dirk's plate. She served nothing for herself, but continued to busy herself at the stove.

Dirk said bleakly, "We will go back to the farm. To come here was a mistake."

Anna gave a deep unhappy sigh. "The farm is now the boys'."

"Yes, well, there is always work for an extra hand. With me to help, they need not pay a hired man."

"And the house—" said Anna softly, "that is the wife's."

"She will be glad of your help and knowledge. Especially when the babies come."

"So different the young folks do things now. . . ." Anna's whisper faded into silence.

Neither she nor Dirk wanted to admit aloud what they knew well; there was no longer any place for them on the farm.

"If"—Anna faltered at last, made daring by hopelessness—"if maybe we *could* talk to the teacher?"

"Hmmmff," Dirk grunted.

The front door opened softly. Footsteps beat a fast light tattoo on the stairs.

"*Joey!*" Dirk roared. "Come down here!"

"Sure, Pa." Slowly the footsteps reversed direction and came closer. Joey appeared sullen-faced in the kitchen doorway.

"Where have you been till this hour?"

"I had to stay after school."

Anna's sharply indrawn breath was a warning. Joey went on quickly, "An' then I went downtown."

"Why?" Dirk demanded.

"I—I was just sort of lookin' around . . ." Joey's scared glance went from Dirk to Anna and back again. What had happened? What had they found out? "Seein' if anybody needed a boy . . . but nobody did . . . so I—I jus' came home."

The silence stretched long as a bridge across the Pacific. Joey's nerves stretched with it.

Then Dirk said, "Sit and eat. Here, give me your jacket; I will hang it up."

Eyes wary as a wild animal's, Joey surrendered the jacket and watched Dirk carry it away. Anna set a heaped plate before him. Joey ate rapidly, scarcely tasting what he put in his mouth.

Dirk returned. He picked up the evening paper and opened it.

Joey said, "I got homework to do."

Nobody stopped him as he streaked for the door and up the stairs. Apparently nothing more was to be said about his late homecoming. But Joey was badly shaken.

Once in his room with the door closed, he slithered under his bed and brought out the watch. Wow! Lucky he'd been able to skid the thing through his doorway before answering Pa's summons! Pa had surely been looking for *something* when he made off with the jacket! But what—and why?

In the kitchen, Dirk said, "He lied. About what, I am not sure, but falsehood was in everything he said. He is a liar and a thief."

"Ah, no!" cried Anna.

"Anna," Dirk said severely, "do you help a broken bone grow straight by saying it is not broken?"

Anna was silent. Dirk bent his head into his hands . . . a sign of helplessness so unusual that Anna looked at him in alarm.

"Tomorrow," said Dirk, "we will talk to his teacher."

Mrs. Meade set an hour for their call when Joey was in a distant class. Round and round they went, seeking the reason for Joey's unsatisfactory school work, his belligerent attitude, his seemingly reasonless lies. Dirk said nothing about the quarrel over Joey's earnings; that was a family matter and, he thought, long ago settled.

"I just don't understand it." Mrs. Meade shook her head at the end of the fruitless discussion. "He should have adjusted to new surroundings by now. Unless—think hard—was there some very special thing he couldn't bring with him from his old home? No? Well, then, has there been something out here that he set his heart on and couldn't have? Sometimes disappointment will cause such a reaction."

Dirk shook his head. Tiredly. Resignedly, "No," he said, "he wants for nothing."

Anna touched his sleeve. Timidly she reminded him, "A dog."

14

ooooooooo

"OH, *YAH*, SURE. A dog," Dirk admitted. "Just a notion the boy got in his head for a while."

Mrs. Meade asked, "You didn't want him to have a dog?"

Dirk frowned. "A fool waste of money, feeding an animal that can do nothing in return but wag its tail! Joey knows that."

"I see," Mrs. Meade said thoughtfully. "But isn't it possible that in this case a dog *could* do something in return? Like helping to solve Joey's problem?"

"All foolishness," grumbled Dirk. "We had no such nonsense to put up with on the farm."

"On the farm Joey was surrounded by animals. Working animals, of course, but to a boy they might well have been friends and companions. Don't you suppose he misses them?"

Dirk shook his head. He felt like a swimmer far beyond his depth. "I don't know what goes on in the boy's head."

Mrs. Meade sighed. "I'm afraid I don't either. His desire for a dog is the only clue we have. Mr. Van Oolbekink, isn't it worth a trial?"

"*Yah, yah,*" Dirk agreed tiredly. "Maybe so. I will see about it."

The day was a long and scary one for Joey. He had been afraid to leave the watch at home—what if Pa took a notion to search his room while he was in school?—yet he was equally afraid to have it in his pocket.

Last night, after his brush with the five-and-dime manager, Joey hadn't dared stop at Barton's store. Sure that the police were after him, he had darted down alleys and through parking lots, not stopping till his breath ran out.

When he was positive he had eluded the chase, he made his cautious way home—only to be met there by his parents' puzzling attitude. Joey didn't know what to think nor what to expect.

Though he jumped like a startled deer every time his name was spoken, the school day passed uneventfully. Promptly at its end Joey went home, not wanting to compound the trouble there by being late another day.

He opened the front door softly. Anna was bustling about the kitchen. From the basement came the rhythmic push-pull of a handsaw (Joey remembered uneasily that sawing wood for the fireplace was one of his own neglected chores).

Nobody appeared to have heard him come in, so

he tiptoed up the stairs to his room. Now was his chance to find a really good hiding place for the watch, someplace where it would be safe from even the most determined searcher till Joey nerved himself for another try at collecting the reward.

He stopped at his dresser to put the watch in a drawer while he sought a better hiding place, but what he saw on the dresser made him forget he was even holding the watch.

Lined up neatly there were his penknife, pencil stubs, bent nail, paperclips, and a smoothed-out sheet of notebook paper, headed "Social Living" with his name in the upper corner. His brain whirled.

If he'd had a hideout, he'd have dived into it. If he'd had a dollar or two, he'd have run away.

But having neither hideout nor cash, he stumbled to the bed and just sat there. Never in his life had he been so scared. What was going to happen next?

Perhaps, after all, his parents had heard him come home, for when supper was ready Anna came to the foot of the stairs—just like any day—and called, "Joey? Come and eat."

Dirk was already at the table when Joey came down the stairs. Dirk never talked much at meals; there was nothing unusual about his silent concentration on the food, but to Joey the wordless minutes were full of menace. He kept waiting for Dirk to clear his throat and push his plate a little from him, as he did before making a serious announcement.

Anna kept up a patter of nervous small talk. How is the schnitzel? Enough pepper? Drink your milk, Joey.

Joey, choking down untasted mouthfuls, said nothing. Nothing at all.

Then the moment came. Dirk pushed his plate away from him. He cleared his throat.

"Joey," he said—Joey's heart missed a beat, then plunged furiously into double time—"how would you like to have a dog?"

"Dog?" Joey echoed.

"Sure, sure, *dog*," Dirk repeated. "Your ma says 'Joey wants a dog, Joey wants a dog'; that's all I hear. Well? Is that how it is?"

Joey said faintly, "I—I guess so." What web was Pa spinning?

"So all right. Saturday we will go to the pound and you can choose yourself a dog."

Joey forgot all about plots and webs and worries and fears. Blood rushed to his head, turning his fair skin beet-red. He threw down his fork with a noisy clatter. "No!" he yelled. "I don't *want* a—a scroungy ol' mutt from the pound! I won't—you can't make me—NO!"

91

15

○○○○○○○○○

DIRK WAS SHOCKED almost beyond words. What kind of answer was that, when he'd just made such a great concession? His face darkened; he half rose, ready to leave the table in anger.

Sight of Anna's pleading eyes made him control his indignation. He forced himself to sit down again and say, "All right, what is it you want, then? For a while it was a dog, but now I suppose it's something else already."

"I do want a dog, I do!" cried Joey. "But a *good* dog—with papers—"

"Papers?"

"—that show how many champions he had for grandparents and great-grandparents! Bob Barton's got an ol' beagle with more ancestors than a—than a king, practically!"

"Ah!" said Dirk. For the first time he saw a glimmer of light beyond this confused maze. "So a friend of yours has such a wonder-dog, *yah?*"

"He's no friend of mine!"

Dirk ignored this. "And where do you obtain these creatures with all the grandparents?"

Joey looked at his father suspiciously. Was he being funny or sarcastic? "At kennels! There's one out on Simmons Road. I used to see their sign on my . . . when I was—" Joey didn't want to mention the lost paper route at a moment like this. He hurried on, "And there's another on Kinney Lane where they sell boxers. And lots more in the ads in the papers!"

Anna held her breath; would Dirk make the right answer?

"*Yah,* well," Dirk said cautiously, "perhaps we will look in at one or two of these places on Saturday."

"Yeh?" Joey's monosyllable was just short of total disbelief.

"Providing, of course, that your chores are done and your homework finished."

Joey pinched himself. Yes, he was awake. "Yeh, sure," he said, "I better get at it right away."

Up in his room everything was just as it had been. The troublesome watch was still in the dresser drawer, reminding him to find a better hiding place. The mysterious line-up of items last seen in the manager's hands at the five-and-dime still faced him on the dresser top. The problem of where to get cash for school supplies and 4-H dues and spending money was as pressing as ever.

Yet through this crushing weight of problems, he'd heard a voice—if his ears were hearing right,

Pa's voice—saying he could have a dog, a real grandson of champions like Bob's beagle! Or anyway that they'd go *look* at them—golly!

For an exciting moment his problems became unimportant, wiped from his mind like chalk marks wiped from the blackboard by the janitor's damp rag.

A dog—a real winner! Not a fat old has-been like that beagle of Bob's, but a sporty pup! Maybe he'd enter it in the dog show at Portland! He pictured himself parading around the ring, the handsome young dog high-stepping beside him . . . or striding forward, regal and erect, to receive the top award, a purple ribbon!

"Yeh, Best in Show," he'd tell the kids at Hopkins, making sure Bob was within hearing. "He's quite a dog, all right. We're thinking of taking him to the nationals!"

Boy, wouldn't that make ol' Bob's eyes bug out? He wouldn't be so much-of-a-much then! Let him have his old House and dog and be a football hero and get moved up to Intermediate Band, like Mr. Frank was promising him today! Joey would more than make up for all that glory with his champion dog.

Wouldn't catch any old ladies calling him a barbarian when he was out walking a dog like that! And if a kid, no matter how big, gave him so much as a dirty look, he'd just say calmly, "I think you'd better know this dog's a fighter. One word from me and he'd be at your throat!"

Lost in daydreams, Joey lay on his bed, hands behind his head. His homework was as forgotten as his crush of problems. He could think of nothing but Saturday.

"Just you wait!" he told the invisible throng that had belittled him. *"You'll* see!"

Saturday came at last. Spurred by last-minute necessity, Joey had rushed through his homework any which way, and made a higgledy-piggledy job of his chores. Dirk kept his comments buttoned behind tight-closed lips; it was a change for the better that the boy had done anything at all.

They drove first to the kennels on Simmons Road. ALBENS' GRAY GHOSTS, said the sign on the gate. Silver-gray Weimaraners, alert but silent, came running to the fence to inspect them. Their light, floating pace, their striking all-over grayness, gave Joey an eerie feeling that the dogs were creatures from another world.

"No puppies right now," their owner said. "But we should have some fine youngsters to show you after Thanksgiving."

As they turned back to the car, Dirk asked, "How much will they be?"

"Well, that depends on the puppy, of course," said Mr. Albens. "The average is around three hundred."

Joey's mouth sagged open. Dirk too was jolted. He managed to say, "I see," before pushing Joey ahead of him into the car. Neither spoke till they were back on the main road, then Joey asked faintly, "Did he say—did he mean—three hundred *dollars?*"

"The man is crazy," Dirk pronounced. "Who would spend money like that for a dog? Where is the next place?"

Joey directed him to Kinney Lane. Here a different reception met them. Stocky, muscular, brindle-colored dogs announced the presence of strangers with deep strong barks that brought the kennel owner from his house. Joey looked at them admiringly; their wide heads and large expressive eyes and mighty chests matched his mental picture of a real dog. Wouldn't a powerhouse like that show up Bob's beagle? Ol' Tex'd take one look and run like a scared rabbit!

Yes, there was a litter of pups of just about an age to leave their mother. Joey would have run to them instantly; Dirk, grown cautious after their first experience, held him back.

"How much are you asking?"

Again the stupefying figures hit their ears like

hammer blows. A hundred fifty and up. One pup, the smallest of the litter, might go for, say, a hundred ten.

"Come along, Joey."

"Aw, *gee*, Pa!"

The kennel owner said, "You aren't going to find purebreds for much less, you know. That little fellow's a real bargain if you're not looking for a show dog."

"*Pa,*" Joey begged, "can't we anyway *look?*"

Dirk turned to stare at him disbelievingly. "For a hundred and ten dollars? *A hundred and ten dollars!*"

"Might make it a hundred," the owner suggested.

But Joey, carried away for a moment by the splendor of his dreams, was back to earth again and sadly aware of the impossibility of such a price. Silently he followed Dirk to the car. Silently they drove away.

"Where now?" Dirk asked a half-mile later.

Joey shook his head. Nowhere would he find the dog he was looking for—the superdog that would make him a superboy—at a price Dirk would pay.

"Home, I guess," he muttered at last. His shoulders hunched, his face grew closed and sullen.

16

oooooooooo

"COME NOW," said Dirk sternly, "no need to look so down in the mouth! There are other places to find a dog."

"Don't want any other dog," Joey mumbled. Memory of the beautiful boxers was more bitter than a spoonful of Anna's spring tonic. But—a hundred dollars!

I've got fifteen of it in my dresser drawer—the thought suddenly struck sparks in his mind. Yes, he had fifteen dollars in his dresser drawer—if he could nerve himself to collect that reward. Would the owner of the boxers take fifteen dollars as a down payment? And if he did, how would Joey find the next payment, and the next? Kids just didn't leave valuable watches on a washbasin *every* day!

Nor a purse full of money in an open locker. If he hadn't put the purse back, how much more would he have? Was the girl who had locker 297 *always* that careless?

Shocked at the direction his thoughts had taken, Joey swerved from that dangerous track to hear Pa saying something about the ads in last night's paper.

"Here, for instance," Dirk concluded as he parked before a pet shop. "With so many to sell, they won't be asking any such fancy price as those kennels."

Halfheartedly, Joey followed his father into the pet shop. The place was a-chatter with sound. Monkeys, parrots, canaries, parakeets, sociable puppies bidding for attention, questioning kittens deciding if they wanted it—altogether they kept up a chorus that drowned out Dirk's and the shopkeeper's discussion. A puppy tried to climb over its mesh enclosure to reach Joey; he scratched its furry stomach, but his thoughts were still with the handsome boxers. Somehow he *would* acquire a dog like that, much finer than Bob Barton's beagle!

The shopkeeper and Dirk came closer. "Now, of course, the price is much less for crossbreeds," the shopkeeper was saying. "Take this litter, for example—" The friendly puppy transferred its attention from Joey to the shopkeeper's pointing finger. "The mother was a purebred wirehaired terrier. The father—well, not a terrier obviously, but the puppies are very cute. We're asking only ten dollars."

"Ten dollars!" Dirk shook his head at the madness of a world where animals of no use wore such price tags. "Enough to paper a room or buy a week's bread and meat!"

The shopkeeper suggested, "There's always the pound. You'll find some good animals in need of a home."

"No!" said Joey.

Dirk frowned to silence him. Reluctantly he reached for his wallet. "Ten dollars," he muttered, "an awful waste! But if that's how it's got to be—"

"*No!*" said Joey, louder than before. How could he compete with Bob if he had only a crossbreed? "Not these either!" The puppy was licking his finger. He jerked his hand away and ran out of the store.

Dirk followed him to the car, his face clouded with rising anger. "What's got into you, boy? Ten dollars I was ready to throw away for nothing—and that doesn't satisfy you?"

Joey slid far down in the car seat; his stubborn chin rested on his chest. "Don' want a dog 'less it's a *good* dog! A purebred."

In dour silence Dirk headed the car for home. He was terribly affronted. Here he'd been ready to spend ten dollars—*ten dollars!*—on a useless animal, and what thanks had he got? His indignation mounted. It was all foolishness, that teacher's notion of how to deal with a misbehaving boy! A good licking would straighten him out faster and cheaper.

But he'd tried that, and where had it got them? Only deeper into a morass of problems.

Dirk heaved a mighty sigh. Tonight, he decided, he would write young Dirk and Teunis, tell them the move had been unwise, and he and Anna and Joey were coming back to the farm. Of course Anna and the new young wife . . . Dirk sighed again. Was there no way out of this thorny tangle without someone being hurt? Well, he would sleep on it tonight and take it to the Lord at Sunday's service. But if the Lord did not come up with an answer, Dirk would—and no later than Monday.

Anna was waiting for them in the front hall. At sight of their identical expressions—jaws tight-set, lips clamped in stubborn lines, frowns like brooding thunderclouds—her own look of happy expectation vanished.

Dirk answered the question she didn't dare ask. "No dog," he said severely, "and no more talk of dogs! Joey, get busy on that woodpile!"

It was a tone of voice that Joey didn't dare disobey. As slow as ice moving out in the spring, he slouched down the basement steps and mutinously sawed at a speed that wouldn't stoke the fireplace for more than one hearth-warming a winter. Intermingled confusingly with his memory of the proud boxers was the feeling of a puppy's fuzzy fur under his hand and the touch of a rough eager tongue. . . .

"Don't want it—no, I don't!" Joey gave the saw a

savage jerk. "What good's a stupid ol' crossbreed?"

The saw twisted and stuck in the log. *Darn ol' saw! Darn ol' log!* Louder than his tormented thoughts rose a small, mournful sound; Joey was startled to realize it came from him. *Cryin', for Pete's sake!* Well, that did it; that was the ever-living end!

Furiously he stamped up the stairs and into the kitchen, where Dirk and Anna sat silently at the table.

"Darn ol' saw's stuck!" he roared, his voice betraying him with a ridiculous upward swoop. "An' I got homework to do anyway! So there!"

Humiliated by the tears that dribbled down his cheeks, Joey marched past his parents and on up to his room. He would run away; yes, that's what he'd do! Just as soon as he collected that reward money. Monday, right after school . . .

"Joey!"

Instinctively Joey clapped his hand to his pocket, sure that the watch glowed through the fabric like powerful radium. The 4-H director was standing at the door of the activities room.

"Oh, hi, Mr. Sanford."

"Joey, have you chosen a project yet?"

"Well, uh—gee, I haven't had time—"

"Let's get it settled right now. Come in and we'll go through the booklet."

Joey gave an anguished look at the big clock face at the end of the hall. The football coach had kept them hard at it till four-thirty. He'd have to really put on steam to reach Barton's store before it closed.

"Well—uh—I got an errand to do—"

"This won't take but a minute. Come on in."

Reluctantly Joey went into the activities room. Mr. Sanford handed him a thick booklet entitled *4-H Project Preview*. Disinterestedly, his mind still on the speeding clock hands, he turned pages. "Gee, I dunno, Mr. Sanford. I don't see nothin' . . ."

"Ever tried woodworking? Leathercraft? How about archery?"

Joey didn't hear him. As he turned the page headed "Livestock," his attention had been caught by a word that fairly leaped at him: "Dogs." He read avidly.

"Hey, what's all this about raising a pup for Guide Dogs? You mean they *give* you a pup?"

Mr. Sanford looked over his shoulder. "Let's see, I have more information on that. . . ."

He went over to the supply cupboard to search through the booklets.

"Here it is, all the details. Want to take these along?"

"Yeh!" Joey's excitement mounted. For a second and third time he read the paragraph that began, "You have been entrusted with a purebred puppy from highly selected breeding stock . . ."

Purebred. Highly selected breeding stock. A puppy as fine as anything out at those kennels— maybe even finer!

"And they'll send it *free?* It won't cost a cent?"

"Well, its care will cost something, of course," Mr. Sanford said. "But the Guide Dog people pay for the puppy's transportation, both ways."

Both ways. In the fever of his inspiration Joey had forgotten that the puppy wouldn't be his to keep. His pulses slowed. Halfheartedly, he poked through the leaflets Mr. Sanford had given him. "Golly, I dunno. I better think about it some more."

"Yes, of course. Talk it over with your parents. It's a fine worthwhile project, and I'm sure you'd qualify—a farm boy like you with a good record of other livestock projects."

"Yeh," said Joey vaguely. The puppies pictured in the booklet hypnotized him. So handsome, alert, intelligent—boy, wouldn't a dog like that make Bob's beagle look like a moth-eaten relic from the rummage shop? "How long d'ya get to keep it?"

"I believe until it's a year old. Certainly you'd have it all the school year."

"Gee . . ." Joey couldn't close the booklet and shut the puppies from his sight. A whole year, practically. Lots of things could happen in a year. If he saved all his money, maybe the Guide Dog folks'd sell the pup to him. Maybe they sent out so many dogs they'd forget he had one, if he kept quiet about it. Surely, given so long a time, he could figure out some way to hang on to the puppy once he had it.

"How quick can I get it?"

"Well, there'll be papers to fill out. They don't trust their puppies to just anyone, you know; these are very special dogs. But I can ask for an application right away. Then if your parents—"

"It'll be okay with them," Joey promised. Once again his pulses began to throb with excitement. "Pa was gonna buy me a dog anyway, but I'd a lot rather have one of these! *Gee*, Mr. Sanford, thanks!"

Clutching his booklets as carefully as if they were printed on gold leaf, Joey left Hopkins. He was within sight of his house before he remembered that he hadn't intended to return home—not ever again! The watch was still heavy in his pocket, as forgotten as all the weekend's detailed planning. Here he'd smuggled extra food out of the house this morning . . . suffered through the day in two sets of underwear, socks, shirts, pants, so he'd have extra for the road! And then in one minute—swish, snap!—he'd forgotten

105

entirely his plan to run away!

But the recollection no sooner entered his mind than it was gone again, chased by the much more important news he was carrying like an Olympic torch.

"Pa! Hey, Pa!" he shouted, slam-banging into the house. "Look what I got—quick, read it! Can I do it, Pa—hey, can I?"

17

ooooooooo

TO DIRK THE change in Joey was startling. It was like sending one boy to school in the morning and having a complete stranger return at night. Though he was ready almost at once to grant Joey's request, he felt it necessary to hem and haw a bit first.

"A dog, *yah?*" he rumbled, leafing through the material Joey had brought home. "And it costs nothing? Hmm, hmm, we must look into this carefully. You don't get something for nothing, you know."

"But you *do*, Pa—that's what it *says*—just read it!"

"Hmmm . . . hmmmm . . . be quiet now, I must be sure the words don't say one thing and mean another—"

"Oh, *Pa!* You *know* it's all right if Mr. Sanford says so!"

"Well, yes . . . hmmm . . . I will give it some thought."

"But I want to know right away! So Mr. Sanford can write 'em—"

"He can't write the letter before tomorrow, can he? Very well, then. I will think about it tonight."

With that, Joey had to be content. Tamping down his excitement and impatience as best he could, he went off to tell Anna about it.

"A real purebred!" he explained in glowing detail. "Like those dogs we saw at the kennels that cost hundreds and hundreds of dollars! Nobody in town'd have a better dog than that—and it wouldn't cost a cent. They *give* it to you, Ma! All you gotta do is promise to take care of it right, and train it a little . . ."

The bubbling overflow of words made little sense to Anna, but she was too happy at the transformation in Joey to care.

"*Ach,* how nice!" she smiled. "How good of them to give such fine puppies away!"

"Well, they don't exactly give 'em away . . . anyway, not right to begin with." Joey didn't try to explain further. The gap between the Guide Dog foster-home plan and his own private intentions couldn't be spanned with a few easy words. "But isn't it *great,* Ma? D'you think Pa'll let me have one? Whyn't you go ask him, huh? Please?"

"Perhaps after supper," she put him off gently.

Restless, Joey went up to his room to change from school clothes. The weight of the watch in his jacket pocket reminded him that he'd figured to be on the highway by now, thumbing a ride east. Was it only yesterday that he'd made all those plans? Absent-mindedly, his mind leaping ahead to speculate on Dirk's decision and what else could be done to influence it, Joey buried the watch deep in a box of summer-weight clothing and shoved the box well back on his closet shelf.

Then, already forgetting its existence, he peeled off the extra layers of clothing that had been so smothering warm all day, got into T-shirt and denims, and hurried downstairs . . .

To fill the woodbox by the fireplace . . .

To set the table for Anna . . .

To polish his shoes—and then Dirk's shoes—and finally Anna's shoes, each gleaming pair fairly shouting "What a good boy am I!"

Just before bedtime Dirk gave his decision. Joey could ask for a Guide Dog puppy, *if*—

The list of "ifs" was long, but Joey was much too delighted to be discouraged by it. Yes (he promised happily in answer to each of Dirk's conditions), he'd apply for another paper route; yes, he'd do his chores faithfully without being reminded; yes, he'd work harder at school; yes, he'd bring his grades up where they belonged; yes, yes, yes!

First thing in the morning, Mr. Sanford was notified, and the request airmailed to Guide Dog headquarters in California. Back came application forms to be filled out. Joey's impatience mounted with his anticipation.

It was almost a welcome relief, these days of marking time, to have Dirk's list of conditions to work at. Never were chores so well and promptly completed, never was homework so diligently studied. It was a little harder to swallow his pride and ask the *Journal* manager for another chance, but Joey did it.

There was a route open, the manager admitted cautiously. It covered a new subdivision; not as many customers as Joey's former run, but more opportunity to solicit new subscriptions. If Joey was interested— and would really work at it. *Sure,* Joey agreed, as he agreed to everything these splendidly thrilling days: *fine, swell—gee, thanks!*

Before Joey's enthusiasm could quite wear him out, the answer came from Guide Dog headquarters. His application had been accepted. The puppy assigned to him was a German shepherd, with the impressive registered name of Count Eric von Hessendorf. Within two weeks Eric would arrive—by air, since Westport was outside the area in which puppies were delivered personally.

All that day Joey floated on his own special cloud. His only anchor to earth was the booklet Mr.

Sanford gave him, *How To Raise Your Guide Dog Puppy*.

"Read it carefully," Mr. Sanford warned. "Make sure you've done everything necessary to get ready for the puppy."

"You bet!" Joey promised. "I sure will!" And he wafted away on his cloud, the unread booklet jammed into his notebook.

Not until evening did he settle down enough to study it. Some of the requirements weren't too bad; the yard already had a dog-tight fence (if nobody left the gate open), and he guessed he could make a dog bed from materials in the basement.

But other items required money. "Light chain . . . suitable dish . . . stiff brush . . . comb." And there'd be dog food to buy.

The matter of money had not been mentioned between Joey and his father since the night of the quarrel. True to his promise, he hadn't asked Dirk for a penny.

Now what was he to do? Was the puppy to scrounge around garbage cans for its food—as Joey had scrounged through lockers for money to buy school supplies?

Memory of the past bad months made Joey's cheeks grow hot. Sneaking, stealing—those awful minutes when he couldn't get rid of the girl's purse; the

111

terrible scare at the five-and-dime—yes, he'd kept his promise not to ask Dirk for money, but right now he couldn't take pride in the fact. If he'd been caught at somebody's locker . . .

"Bet those Guide Dog folks'd never have let me have a puppy *then!*" Joey shivered at thought of how close he'd come to spoiling everything. No sir—no more of that! Just let someone even suspect he was stealing, and—*wham, socko!*—there'd go the puppy, fast as the authorities could swoop down and snatch it away.

Joey frowned hard at the booklet. Then with sudden resolution he took it with him downstairs where Dirk sat reading his *Farmer's Weekly* while Anna, beside him, rocked gently as she darned socks.

Joey took a deep breath. Here it came.

"Pa," he said, the word booming out louder than he'd intended and very firm, "there's things I gotta buy for the puppy 'fore it comes—an' then there'll be dog food an' stuff. Looks like I'll need some of my money."

There. He'd said it. Broken his promise, humbled himself to make the request. Only, strangely, he didn't *feel* humble! As a matter of fact, he felt good.

Dirk laid down his magazine. He nodded gravely. The tone of his voice was very man-to-man as he said, "Well, now, better we get pencil and paper and figure how much it will take."

Some of the lines eased out of Anna's face. As she rocked and darned, she hummed a tuneless little song. A log shifted in the fireplace, sending up a shower of sparks and a cheerful crackle to add to Anna's song. Dirk's and Joey's voices blended in a businesslike murmur. Rain dripped against the windows, but inside the Van Oolbekink house was the enveloping warmth of a summer day.

On a Saturday afternoon two weeks later Dirk drove Joey to the airport. Joey's heart pounded as the plane from the south circled and swooped in for a landing. Certainly it took hours, he thought impatiently, for the passengers to get off, for the baggage to be unloaded and brought into the station. He darted back and forth behind the passengers who blocked his view of the luggage pickup counter. Had the puppy come? Was it all right?

Then he heard a small, troubled whine. The sound was a magnet; it pulled him through the line of grown-ups like a sliver of metal slicing through butter—

Straight to the special airline pet-carrier from whose wire sides a black nose poked out.

All the breath went out of Joey. He could do nothing but stand there, blocking the luggage counter, grinning wider than a clown in a circus.

Dirk appeared beside him. "So he is here," he said, presenting his claim check for the carrier.

"Yeh," murmured Joey. Tentatively he put a finger to the wires. The black nose sniffed it; a pink tongue came forward and licked it. "Yeh!" repeated Joey in loud delight. "He's here!"

III

○○○○○○○○○

Time
of Change

18

oooooooooo

DURING THE TWO weeks of waiting for Eric, Joey's conceit had puffed to the proportions of a County Fair balloon. Now at last he would be recognized as Somebody. The handsome purebred dog, soon to be his, would surely make those know-it-all kids at Hopkins sit up and take notice. Nowhere in Westport—and that included the House!—was there a dog bred of finer stock.

"German shepherd," he bragged to everyone he could hold still long enough to listen. "Name's Eric. Count Eric von Hessendorf. Pedigree longer'n my arm, and more famous ancestors than—than the Queen of England, practic'ly!"

By the end of two weeks Joey was finding it difficult to pin down listeners. When they saw Joey coming, they ducked around corners or busied themselves at their lockers or escaped with a muttered, "Gotta get somethin' 'fore next class."

Joey wasn't rebuffed. He either failed to notice the slight or charged it to jealousy. Excitedly he strutted and boasted and swaggered his way through the days till the fateful Saturday.

Now Eric was here.

Sitting close beside the pet carrier on the ride home, Joey was filled with happiness. Again and again he slipped his finger through the wires, stroked the velvet-soft nose thrust forward to investigate it, shivered with delight when the puppy trustfully licked it.

"Hey, Pa, I think he likes me!"

"*Yah*, sure."

"I bet he knows a'ready I'm his friend. He's real smart—you can tell jus' by lookin' at him."

"*Yah*, we see once how many messes you clean up. Then we know how smart he is."

"I betcha he learns right away! I betcha he'll be paper-broke by—by tomorrow morning! I betcha—"

"Big talk slices no onions."

"Well, you'll see!"

"*Yah*, we'll see."

When at last they were in the yard at home with the gate tightly shut, Joey opened the carrier and released Eric.

The three-month-old puppy was as appealing as a teddy bear. His thick coat, gray with black-and-tan markings, still retained its puppy texture of cotton-wool. His paws were hugely out of proportion, like a clown's oversize shoes, making his legs look stubby by comparison. He walked out of the carrier with a slightly rolling gait, then sat down suddenly in a graceless heap as though the paws had proved just too enormous to move. One ear stood perkily erect; the other lopped over.

"Oh, golly!" cried Joey, his heart spilling over with joy and pride. "Isn't he *beautiful?*"

Eric understood the tone, if not the words. He thumped his tail in vigorous agreement; his brown eyes—surely, thought Joey, the brightest, smartest eyes that ever looked out of a dog's face!—laughed with approval. He rose and shook himself, a complicated process that started with his ears and went on to include head, shoulders and rump, and ended with rapidly switching tail. This done, he trotted off with his ridiculous side-to-side roll on a tour of investigation . . .

Straight toward the garden where Dirk's winter crop of pumpkins and gourds gleamed gold and shiny green among the tangled vines.

"Stop him!" roared Dirk. "He'll dig up the vines! He'll—look at that! The rascal's got one of my gourds!"

"Eric!" yelled Joey. He plunged over the plowed ground. The puppy had pounced on the hard-shelled gourd as though on a marrow-bone and was now trying to carry it off, vine and all. "Eric, drop it!"

Eric had no intention of giving up his treasure.

119

Legs braced, big paws firmly planted, he tugged at the vine with short sharp jerks, growling all the while like a miniature volcano.

Not until Joey was close enough to grab for him did the puppy abandon his prize. Then he headed for the house where Anna had appeared on the porch steps. On his way to meet her Eric took a shortcut through her zinnias (where he paused to scratch up a small patch of ground and sniff it vigorously) and relieved himself beside her most splendid chrysanthemum.

"No, no!" cried Anna—too late. "*Ach,* he knows no better. Quick, Joey, get the shovel!"

"And the spade," directed Dirk. "Maybe we can yet save the vine. *Ach,* that pup, he's a bad one!"

"No, he isn't!" Joey protested. "It's my fault. I shoulda kept him on leash—the book said to show him right away where his bathroom was. You can't blame *him.*"

"Hmmph," Dirk muttered, frowning over his damaged garden. "Well, we'll see. There's training needed somewhere, that's plain."

Considerably shaken, Joey attached the leash to Eric's collar and led him to the kitchen for water and his first meal.

"You see what you did, Eric? First crack outa the box, you went and got me in a peck of trouble!

Now you gotta behave, understand?"

Eric wagged obligingly as he wolfed the carefully measured ration of kibbled food set before him, then slurped up water as though coming upon an unexpected oasis after a long desert march.

"Oh, boy," sighed Joey, thinking of the chrysanthemum accident still to be disposed of, "I better show you your bathroom *quick!* You sure gotta lot to learn, boy."

And until he learned it, Joey had to work fast and hard. First off, the yard. Plainly he couldn't leave Eric free to do his worst during the school day. Why, in just the time it would take to deliver his *Journal*s, Eric could make a shamble of Anna's flowers and Dirk's garden!

"He'll have to have a run," Joey decided worriedly. But a run would take time to build—and more money.

"A little chicken wire from the garage to the fence, that will do it," said Dirk as though reading Joey's thoughts. "The roll in the basement should be enough. Tomorrow we put it up. For now, a rope to the clothesline, *yah?*"

"Yeh," said Joey gratefully. "Won't take him long to learn what he shouldn't do! You'll see."

"*Yah*, I wait," said Dirk.

It was hard to leave Eric behind when the time

121

came to deliver papers. The puppy strained at the end of his rope, and whimpered as forlornly as though Joey were abandoning him.

"Pretty quick I'll figure a way so you can go along too," Joey promised him. The puppy's whimpers echoed in his ears and speeded his pace. Until he reached home again, he couldn't quite believe that Eric would survive his absence.

Eric's actions indicated that he too had thought it unlikely. At sight of Joey he bounced to the end of the rope and set up a hallelujah of puppy barks. Joey knelt and hugged his new friend. "Gee, Eric, you better get housebroken awful fast," he told the puppy, " 'cause I wanta take you to school some 4-H day soon; boy, won't you rock 'em back on their heels? But you got to know how to behave first."

Start training the second day without fail.

First thing Sunday morning, Joey and Eric went out to the yard to begin work.

"All right now, let's get serious," Joey warned the puppy, who showed more interest in sniffing squirrel trails than following orders. He sat Eric down firmly at his left side. "You been doin' this for weeks a'ready, the book says, so quit actin' like it's brand-new. Okay now. Eric!"

122

The puppy yawned and glanced casually toward the house where a curtain had just moved at a downstairs window. Joey restrained his impulse to give the leash an impatient yank. "That's right. You don't know your name yet, do you, boy? Golly, there's so *much* you gotta learn!"

Not only his name, but housebreaking, retrieving, the commands to heel, sit, come, fetch. To compete with a show dog like Bob's beagle, Eric must know all this and more. And in addition to the training, Joey must feed and exercise the dog, keep him clean and healthy, provide warm, dry, draft-free quarters, make sure there were no more incidents like yesterday's in the garden.

"Golly," said Joey, awed and a little scared at the size of the job he'd undertaken, "you *better* be smart, Eric!"

Eric looked up at him, mouth stretched in a wide grin. He took a length of leash between his teeth and shook it with playful vigor. In puppy language as plain as words he was saying, "Okay, okay, let's get at it!"

Joey laughed aloud. His confidence came rushing back. "You tell 'em, Eric," he agreed cheerfully. "*'Course* we can do it!"

19

ooooooooo

JOEY'S DAY SETTLED slowly, and sometimes a bit bumpily, into the new routine. The first bump was to get up an hour earlier in the morning so he could take Eric out for a run, then prepare the puppy's breakfast before sitting down to his own.

Eric's feeding instructions were tacked to the windowsill above the kitchen counter. Anna read them disbelievingly. She told Dirk, "You should see once—a receipt like out of a cookbook! For a *dog!*"

Nor would Joey depart one iota from the required measurements. "A teaspoon of bacon drippings" meant exactly what it said. When Anna would have poured a dollop from the skillet, he stopped her with a shocked, "Whatcha *doin'?* I gotta *measure* it!"

"*Ach,* you think I don't know how much is a spoonful?" protested Anna, whose recipes had long ago been simplified to a dab of this and a handful of that.

"It's gotta be *accurate,*" Joey insisted stubbornly. He would allow no shortcuts in the care and training of this prize that he counted on to bring him much glory. "Eric's a very special dog."

"But you and Pa, you are not very special people," Anna teased him gently, "so it's all right if I cook for you my own way?"

"Aw, gee, Ma!"

There were a few mornings when Joey would have been glad of her help. Twice he overslept, and once he had homework to finish that he'd neglected the evening before. With frantic glances at the clock's speeding hands, Joey rattled about the kitchen faster than corn in a popper.

"Go eat your breakfast," Anna urged. "I will feed the doggy."

Joey was tempted, but—no, she'd measure the chopped meat by eye and the kibbled food by the handful and probably skip the cod-liver oil and vitamins entirely! Faithfully, painstakingly, Joey prepared breakfast for his impatient puppy, even when it meant missing his own.

Three times was enough, though. After that, Joey made sure his homework was finished before bedtime. As for oversleeping, he cured that by moving Eric's bed from the back entry to his bedroom.

Anna protested, *"Na, na,* no dogs on my good quilt!"

"Eric won't get on the bed, Ma. He's gonna be trained not to get on any furniture."

" 'Going to be' gathers no berries today!"

"Well, he *can't* jump on the bed, Ma, 'cause he can't reach it. I'm gonna do like the book says an' put this screw in the wall behind his bed to fasten his chain to—that's why they said to buy a chain—an' then he can't go any farther than the chain lets him."

Anna frowned disapprovingly. "A chain is not kind."

"Aw, gee, look—it's real light. An' there's a swivel in it so he can move around easy 'thout gettin' tangled. But he can't go any farther from his bed than his papers."

"Papers." Anna's disapproval shifted to a new target. "The room will smell."

"Not very long it won't!" Joey declared proudly. "Two mornings now he's waited for me to take him out. If I get up early enough, it'll soon be *every* morning!"

"*Ach*, well . . ." Anna covered her retreat with a barrage of warnings. "You clear the dirty papers out quick a minute, you hear? And no lying abed while the doggy sniffs about. And leave the window open a crack day and night!"

"Yes, Ma. No, Ma. Sure, Ma." Joey whistled as he prepared Eric's new quarters. It would be fun to have the dog sleeping in his room, a companion in the long silent nights.

Certainly when Eric joined him, there was no

more oversleeping! Now Joey could not silence the noisy alarm with one sleepy groping hand, then snuggle back under the warm covers for an extra snooze. At the first *br-r-r-ring* Eric was on his feet. He woofed and leaped and clattered his chain. The alarm was a lurking enemy, a snake with a huge rattle, and Eric had to protect Joey from its terrible threat. Unable to reach it, he barked deafeningly.

"Hey, look, it's just a little ol' clock," Joey tried to explain. He put the clock on the floor by Eric.

Eric sprang backward. Cautiously, hackles bristling, he stretched his neck till he could sniff the clock. He came closer, sniffed more vigorously, tipped it over. The alarm gave a faint whirr. Eric pounced. His puppy teeth closed on the cold metal, and he shook it fiercely.

Weak with laughter, Joey rescued the clock and put it back on the table. Eric, satisfied that his enemy was dead, paid no further attention to it till the next morning when—*br-r-r-ring!*—it was once more alive and shrilling and needing to be subdued.

"*Grrrrrowf, rowf!*" he thundered. *Rattle-clickity-clatter* went the chain. From his parents' room across the hall came Dirk's stirrings and mutterings. Hurriedly Joey stilled the alarm and his noisy defender.

After that, far from taking an extra snooze, Joey was more apt to hop out of bed *before* the alarm went off and so forestall waking the entire neighborhood.

Eric's training, even more than his feeding, was something Joey couldn't delegate to other hands. Who else would know exactly the right words to use—always the same word for the same command?

"Here, doggy!" Anna tried to coax the puppy to her one day.

"You don't *say* that!" Joey protested. "You gotta say 'Eric—come!' "

"Well, if he comes, what difference?" Anna asked.

"*Plenty* of difference! You gotta use the exactly same words every time. The book says, 'Be consistent.' " Consistency was fast becoming the eleventh commandment in Joey's lexicon.

And good manners the twelfth.

"A well-mannered Guide Dog reflects your consistent attention to details." That's what the book said and Joey lived by the book. A well-mannered Guide Dog stays off furniture, beds, automobile seats . . . is not fed tidbits from the table . . . does not jump on people.

"Eric—sit!" Left hand across the puppy's hips, right hand on his chest, hands pressing gently toward each other.

This was a command Eric had learned before he

left the kennel. It took only a little patient reminding before Joey could apply just the left hand, then very soon do no more than speak the words. "Eric"—count three under his breath to give the dog time to hear and pay attention—"sit!"

"Eric—heel!" Always have him sit first, the book said, then give the command to heel and step forward briskly. Left foot first, *always the left foot first*. And walk fast! A steady quick pace gave the puppy less chance to zigzag in front of his master or be distracted by interesting sights and sounds and scents.

Up and down the yard, up and down Orchard Lane, round and round the long suburban blocks went Joey and Eric, executing right and left turns with growing precision. "No!" when Eric tried to cross in front of him. "Good dog" as the puppy resumed his position close at Joey's left side, shoulders just ahead of Joey's knee. "Eric—sit!" whenever they came to a halt.

Eric loved it all. His wide grin and lolling tongue, as he sat at rest, proclaimed his pleasure in the workouts, the praise, and especially in Joey. He took the leash between his teeth and tugged it to encourage Joey to do more.

It was always Joey who was first out of breath. "Gee, I got about as much wind as a chicken," he grumbled as once more he dribbled to a halt, panting, "Eric"—puff, puff—"sit!" Look, even the pup was laughing at him!

Maybe he *ought* to shift to track, like the football coach was always telling him to do. Tentatively Joey considered the idea. Running—even in those sissy shorts—wouldn't be so bad with Eric running beside him; he could see them clicking off practice miles through the twilight or the early-morning mists. . . .

Certainly most anything would be more fun than football! Sulking on the bench, glowering at Bob Barton's heroics, longing for a chance to emulate them—getting hauled out of a game as fast as he got in, the wind knocked out of him, ribs crunched in, the coach sizzling like steak on a hot platter because he'd tackled instead of sidestepped . . .

Yeh, maybe he just would go talk to the track coach.

"Eric—stay!"

That was the hardest command to teach. Eric wanted to be with Joey as much as Joey wanted to be with Eric. To tell the dog to "stay" and to walk away from him, hearing that small anxious whine as Eric uncertainly remained at "sit," took steely determination. At first Joey walked only the length of the leash, then turned. Eric sat where he had been left, a worried furrow between his eyes, his ears tilted alertly forward.

"Eric—come!" Ah, that was the good moment! The tone of Joey's voice, even more than the slight tug on the leash, told the puppy that all was well and once more he could be at his master's side.

Retrieving, of course, was the most fun of all. This was a game, but like any game it had its rules. "Eric—come!" and the puppy, head high, came dancing with the old rolled-up felt hat of Dirk's that had become Eric's dearest treasure. "Eric—out!" and he must surrender it, his reluctance to give it up eased by the promptness with which Joey threw it again.

Each schoolday, after the morning meal and workout, Joey had to put Eric in his enclosure and leave him. The puppy ran along the fence, following Joey to the farthest corner. The picture of him sitting there, whining softly, black nose thrust between the pickets, stayed in Joey's mind all day and hurried him home in the afternoon.

"Ah, now, he's not lonely," Anna assured Joey. "Your pa talks to him while he works in the yard. And he has squirrels to chase—and today, Mrs. Wickshire's cat!" Anna clucked at the remembrance. "Such squawling you wouldn't believe! If it were any but such a fine lady's cat, I would say it swore at the puppy. Your pa got himself a nice mess of scratches, getting it off the garage roof."

"Aw, it woulda got down by itself."

"Mrs. Wickshire didn't think so. She would have called the firemen to come with their ladders and trample our yard and frighten the doggy—"

Joey frowned. What worried him wasn't the idea of Eric being scared—Eric would have loved the excitement!—but the thought of all the traffic in and out of the dog's enclosure. The portion of yard assigned to Eric included the gate. What if some visitor or salesman or delivery boy left the gate open?

"*Ach*, I watch out good for the doggy!" Anna said positively. "Whenever somebody comes, I look first to see if the gate is closed." But Joey knew Eric could be out of the gate and far away before the caller ever punched the doorbell.

What was needed was more chicken wire, another length to quarter the yard and allow no entrance to Eric's enclosure except through the garage. As soon as he earned enough from the new paper route, Joey planned to buy more fencing. In the meantime . . . he just hoped Mrs. Wickshire and her cat and all other busybodies would stay home!

Eric's response to his first month of obedience training had been splendid. Joey made up his mind to take the dog to the next general 4-H meeting,

Friday afternoon. What a demonstration they would put on!

"But we got to work extra hard this week," he told the puppy. There was an edge to his voice as he issued the familiar commands; his "no" was sharper, his praise more rare. When Eric brought the old felt hat and wagged enticingly, Joey said, "No goofin' off now!" Boy, were they going to show those kids a performance! This was *one* time he wouldn't come off second best to Bob Barton.

Joey planned to make a quick trip home before activity hour Friday to get Eric. In preparation he combed and brushed Eric that morning till the puppy's coat shone like silk, cleaned his ears and eyes with a damp cloth, even washed his paws.

"Now stay clean!" he said sternly as he turned the dog loose in his enclosure. Eric didn't understand the order, and he was troubled by the severity of Joey's tone. What had he done wrong? He followed the boy along the fence line, whining questioningly.

Joey didn't stop at the far corner, as he usually did, to reach between the pickets and pat Eric and say, "Be a good dog. I'll be home soon." Joey's mind was on the 4-H meeting, picturing the triumph he would have.

Eric whined louder as Joey's bike disappeared

down the block. He ran up and down the fence line, looking for a space wide enough to squeeze through. Not finding any, he reared on his hind legs at the gate and pawed vainly at the latch. Again and again he returned to the corner from which he had last glimpsed Joey. At last he lay down there, nose between the pickets, watching, waiting.

Dirk saw him there when he went out to choose a fine squash for Anna to bake. Anna saw him there when she came to the back door to shake her dust mop. The milkman, the bread-truck driver, the mailman saw him there and carefully closed the gate before and after making their deliveries.

A stranger leaving samples of a new product at every house on Orchard Lane did *not* see him. He left the gate unlatched while he hurried up the walk to put his sample on the porch. When he went on to the next house, he closed the Van Oolbekink gate behind him.

20

ooooooooo

"ERIC!" JOEY SENT his clear whistle ahead of him as he sped toward 760 Orchard Lane. "Eric—come, boy!"

Ever since Eric's arrival, Joey had been building toward this moment when he could show the dog off to his schoolmates. Now the stage was set; the audience was waiting.

"Eric!" Usually the big puppy came bouncing to the fence at first sound of Joey's whistle. "Where are you, boy?"

Keeping Mrs. Wickshire's cat corralled in a tree, maybe. Joey leaned his bike against the fence and unlatched the gate. "Hey, Eric!"

Unbelievably, the yard was empty. Surely Anna hadn't let him into the house—unless somehow he'd been hurt? Joey pounded up the steps. "Ma! What's happened to Eric?"

Anna came running, her round face startled. "Joey, you are home so early—*ach*, yes, to get the doggy, of course! All morning he watched for you in that corner—"

135

"He's not there, Ma! He's not anyplace in the yard! The gate was closed, but—"

"*Yah*, sure! I look at it every time after someone comes." Anxiously the two of them hurried outside. Joey's flying feet kicked aside the plastic-wrapped box at the top of the steps, but Anna stooped to pick it up. " 'Free Sample,' " she read from the attached card. "*Ach*, Joey, he did not ring, whoever brought this! I did not know—"

Joey gave her a stricken look. "But then Eric . . . he could be—'most anywhere!" The thought catapulted him toward his bike.

"Wait, Joey—I call your pa! In the car is faster!"

"He can go 'round the streets!" Joey shouted back. "I'll go through alleys. . . . Eric!" Anna heard his shrill whistle long after he was out of sight.

Dirk, roused from his afternoon nap, joined the search in his car. Anna could do nothing to help but make repeated trips from one fence to the other, peering up and down the street, hopefully calling, "Here doggy, doggy!"

Mrs. Wickshire peered over the fence dividing their properties. "Is there trouble?"

"The boy's dog is gone! *Ach*, it is my fault; I did not see the gate was open!"

"Mmmph!" Mrs. Wickshire, thinking of her cat,

looked ready to snap, "Good riddance!" However, she thought better of it and said, "Have you called the pound?"

"The pound? But the dog catcher would not take *our* doggy. He wears his collar always—"

"If he's lost, that's where he'd be taken till someone claimed him."

"Ah, thank you, thank you!" Anna's heart lightened; now she could do something to help. "I will go call right away!"

She was looking up the number of the Humane Society when there was a quick rap on the screen door. Mrs. Wickshire peered in at her. "The veterinarians," she said. "Call them, too. If the dog was hurt, somebody would take him to a vet. That's what happened when my Prunella was hit by a car."

"Ah, you are so kind!" Anna said gratefully.

"I'll look up numbers while you call." Mrs. Wickshire was a born organizer, and here was a situation plainly needing her best efforts. Briskly (for the first time since the Van Oolbekinks' arrival) she entered Anna's home and took immediate charge.

There was no dog of Eric's description at the pound. Nor had any such dog been brought to the first vet they called, or the second. Before Anna could dial another number, the phone rang. She answered eagerly.

It was Mr. Sanford phoning from Hopkins. "Mrs. Van Oolbekink? We're wondering what's keeping Joey. He went home to get his dog—"

"*Ach*, poor Joey, the doggy is gone!" Sorrowfully Anna related the happenings of the afternoon. "Now Joey and his pa, they look for him, the poor lost puppy—"

"That's a shame!" Mr. Sanford's voice was warmly concerned. "Tell you what. I'll dismiss the group and they can all help look. He might very well be in the Hopkins area, you know; he may have picked up Joey's scent and tried to follow him."

That's exactly what Eric had done. When the stranger left the gate unlatched, Eric had needed only a moment to whisk through the opening and, nose to the ground, make off in the direction Joey had disappeared.

The trouble was, a bicycle didn't leave a scent he could follow. Joey's foot had touched ground at the corner where he'd waited for a green light. Eric sniffed excitedly at this proof that he was on his master's trail. But a block later Joey had taken to the street, and the gasoline scent of passing cars covered what further traces Eric's keen nose might have found.

Eric went up one block and down another. He snuffled grass and sidewalk and telephone poles and

138

curbing. Cars honked at him, sending him skittering out of the street. At long last he gave up hope of overtaking Joey and turned toward home.

Following his own trail gave him no trouble. In spite of a detour after a frisky squirrel and an occasional pause to establish friendly relations with another dog, Eric made it home in good time . . .

To find the gate closed.

Eric pawed at it. He was thirsty and he wanted to get to his water pan. The gate proved as hard to get into as it had been to get out of. Eric trotted along the fence. The big gate across the driveway was closed too. His whole yard was closed against him. Eric whined. He curved a paw around one bar of the big gate and shook it. He barked. In the house Dirk napped and Anna rocked and hummed and stitched quilt patches while she listened to the radio. Nobody heard Eric.

Eric sniffed the air. Now his questing nose searched for water. If he couldn't reach his own pan, he'd find a drink somewhere else. It had rained the night before; the shallow puddles were dry by now, but Eric found a deeper one in the alley. Before he could drink from it, a delivery truck came racketing toward him. Eric jumped aside. The truck wheels went through the puddle—*splosh!* Muddy water drenched Eric. He shook himself vigorously, then trotted on to find a cleaner puddle.

His nose led him across a back yard to porch steps where a pan, left out overnight, had caught some of the rain water. Eric lapped it thirstily. A woman came out the door, crying, "Oh, you dirty dog! Look what you've done!" She snatched up the pan of water and emptied it over the muddy footprints on her steps. Quite a lot of it landed on Eric.

Eric decided he'd had enough water. He shook as much out of his coat as he could, spraying the sidewalk with gray drops. The woman rushed down the steps, flourishing a broom, so Eric decided he'd had enough of that house, too.

He trotted rapidly across yards till he came to a sawdust pile outside an open basement window. The sawdust looked pleasantly dry; Eric rolled and rolled in it. The man of the house, returning from his tool-shed with a shovel, ready to scoop the sawdust into his furnace cellar, yelled and swung the shovel. Eric scrabbled out of the pile, scattering sawdust in a powdery cloud and leaving a block-long trail of muddy chips.

Eric's wet nose was caked with mud and sawdust. He sneezed and sneezed. Even if he'd wanted to traverse that unfriendly territory again, he couldn't retrace his trail now, for all he could smell was sawdust.

Big dogs hurried him on with warning barks. A small boy chased him. Cars honked at him. His coat was itchy from drying mud; one paw had been cut by broken glass. Head down, limping, his tail between his legs, Eric plodded on. Traffic was thicker now. There was no soft grass underfoot. He kept to the sidewalk, close to the buildings, out of people's way.

"Scat!" said a man when Eric tried to rest in his store entrance.

"Shoo!" said a restaurant manager when Eric sniffed hopefully at his door.

"Beat it, dog!" . . . "Get outa here!" . . . "On your way, pup!" Where could he find a quiet place to sit down and lick his paw?

Here was an open door. Eric slunk inside. . . .

After Mr. Sanford's phone call, the 4-H club members divided the surrounding neighborhood among themselves and set off in pairs to look for Joey's dog. Mr. Sanford took the farthest section since he had a car to help shorten the distance. Bob Barton went along with Mr. Sanford.

They covered every street slowly, whistling, calling. While Mr. Sanford drove around a block, Bob hiked down the alley that bisected it, looking into every back yard. Nowhere did they spot a dog answering Eric's description.

141

At last they were so far from Hopkins that they had reached the business section of town.

"Might as well call a halt," said Mr. Sanford, "and hope the others had better luck."

"Let's try one more block," Bob urged. "He *could* have gotten this far."

"Not very likely. . . . Well, okay. We'll go the length of Main. I'll watch the right side; you hop out and cover the left."

It was easy to spot a stray in the business section where all non-lost dogs were on leash. Mr. Sanford drove slowly. Bob could almost keep up with him, even with an occasional sortie down an alley.

Unexpectedly, when both were stopped by a red light, they saw Joey hot-footing it down Main toward them!

"Hey, Joey!" yelled Bob. The light changed; he charged across the street. "Any news of him?"

"They got a dog at the police station!" Joey panted. "Sounds like Eric!"

"The *police* station! What'd they do—arrest him?"

"Nope—they said the dog walked in like he knew he was lost! Ma just happened to call 'em; she and a neighbor've been phonin' everybody. . . .Where is it anyway? Pa parked as close as he could get—"

"Back up here—you passed it—c'mon! Hey, Mr.

Sanford!" Bob wigwagged violently and pointed. Mr. Sanford nosed toward a parking place.

The two boys burst into the police station. There, tethered to a desk, sat a half-grown dog. His shoulders drooped, his coat was mud-caked, one paw was bandaged with a handkerchief. He looked about as tired and footsore and lost and sad as a dog could be.

"Eric!" cried Joey, his whole heart in his voice. "Oh, Eric!"

The dog raised his head. His ears perked up. His mouth opened in a wide delighted grin. *"Ruff, ruff, ruff!"* He announced to the world and the smiling police officers that he was no longer a lost dog.

Joey knelt on the floor beside the dog and hugged him hard. "Chee, what's the big idea!" he scolded and hugged at the same time. "Runnin' off like you didn't know better! Boy, are you a mess!"

Ruefully, for the first time, Joey remembered how beautifully he'd groomed Eric for today's show at Hopkins—and especially for Bob Barton! The guy was probably laughing himself sick at all Joey's big talk! Well, let him laugh—Joey didn't care. Not now. Not with his dog back safe in his arms.

Defensively he looked up at his long-time antagonist, ready to say, "Y'oughta see him when he's all cleaned up."

But the words were never spoken. The look on

143

Bob Barton's face made them unnecessary.

"Golly!" said Bob. There was admiration and love and profound respect in the single word. He knelt beside Eric and stroked the matted gray fur. "Isn't he a *beauty!*"

21

ooooooooo

IT WAS THE MOST surprising thing.

When Joey strutted and boasted and tried to prove he was Somebody, kids laughed and called him the Kink. When he bragged up Eric as the smartest, handsomest, most regal dog in Westport, they weren't impressed; they were bored.

But when Eric was lost and Joey in sad trouble, the whole 4-H group turned out to help him. And when the puppy was found—looking not at all royal, but as dirty and dejected as any alley tramp—he won Bob Barton's warmest praise!

Nor did the surprises end there.

After Eric's recovery, anyone would think he belonged to the entire 4-H Club. Every member had taken part in the search; now each one took a proprietary interest in the puppy's welfare.

"How's Eric today—okay?"

"Boy, that pup's smarter'n most kids! *He* knew where to go when he was lost!"

"You gonna bring Eric to the next meeting? Aw, shucks, won't be another till after Thanksgiving!"

Many of the group found that too long to wait to

see the dog that had become theirs. Singly or by twos and threes, they found errands to do in the neighborhood of 760 Orchard Lane. And once there, they hung over the fence to pet Eric and admire him and even accompany Joey and the dog on their brisk walks.

When on one such walk, they met a Hopkins eighth grader who laughed and said, "Well, if it isn't the Kink and his Wonder Dog!" it was Joey's companions who bristled: "Watch out who you're callin' names!" True, it was Eric they were defending, not Joey, but the umbrella of their protection covered both.

After the scene in the police station, a sort of wary truce developed between Joey and Bob Barton. To Joey, Bob was still Bob—a lordly know-it-all, insufferable teacher's pet and football hero—but somehow their scrappy exchanges occurred less often and rarely went beyond words.

One reason, of course, was that there were fewer places for them to clash. Bob had been moved up to Intermediate Band; Joey was still banging away in desultory fashion with the Beginners. Competition in classwork had pretty well evened up, now that Joey was ticking off homework and assignments with unfailing regularity. And the sharpest conflict had disappeared with Joey's exit from football.

It happened the week after Eric's adventure. Joey—elaborately casual, his mind not quite made up —approached the track-and-field coach, Mr. Dedham, as he came off the hockey field. Said Joey, "Figgered maybe I'd like to do some runnin'. Too many kids out for football—not much fun."

Mr. Dedham was a big muscular man with a hearty voice and a handshake like canyon walls closing in on one's bones. "Fine, Joey!" he boomed. "We'll get you started in the jogging program. You'll be fit as a fiddle, come spring training."

"Jogging?" To Joey, jogging was the heavy-footed pace of farm horses as they lumbered toward the barn. "Gee, I guess maybe I don't wanta—"

"Best conditioner I know of," the coach said firmly. "Got the idea when I was in New Zealand last year. *Everybody* jogs Down Under. Boys, girls, businessmen, grandmothers—"

Joey was silent.

"You want to start out easy," Mr. Dedham instructed him. "Walk fifty-five yards, jog fifty-five yards . . . take your time."

This was less and less Joey's idea of a fleet-footed Mercury skimming over the hills. Perhaps he'd just better go back to football. . . .

"Now remember, there's a right way and a wrong way to jog," Mr. Dedham was continuing enthusiastically. "Let's see you chug off a few yards."

"Guy must be nuts," thought Joey. "Any kid knows how to run." Disdainfully, head tucked between his shoulders, elbows clamped to his sides, Joey leaned far forward on his toes and took off.

When he circled back, Mr. Dedham was shaking his head. Slowly, sadly, sympathetically. "All wrong," he said. "Keep erect—loosen up, you're too tense—take short, comfortable steps. Come down flat-footed or on your heel, your foot right beneath your knee, not a yard behind it. Watch!"

Joey could more easily picture the big man as a shot putter or a discus thrower than a runner. But when Mr. Dedham took off across the hockey field, his slow, easy jogging stride made him look light as dandelion fluff drifting on a breeze. He crossed the field and returned, not even breathing faster.

"Pick up a copy of the jogging schedule at my office," he told Joey. "We begin with a mile a day, half jogging, half walking. In twelve weeks you'll be stepping off two and a half miles, steady Fartlek."

"Steady—huh?"

"Steady Fartlek. That's New Zealand talk; means jogging at a speed you can keep up comfortably for more than five minutes."

"Oh—uh—sure." The coach was nuts all right, Joey decided, heading back to his locker for books and jacket—but in kind of a nice way. Once out of sight of the hockey field, he tried to duplicate that light, floating pace.

"An' you know what?" he told Eric that evening as they toured the block. "You really do float—sort of!" Joey eyed the puppy's effortless gait and added in surprise, "Hey, you're a pretty good jogger yourself! Bet if I told you that's steady Fartlek you're doin', you'd act like you knew it all the time!"

During Thanksgiving vacation other 4-H members found their way to 760 Orchard Lane. On Saturday even Bob Barton appeared. He didn't invent an errand to account for his presence in the neighborhood; he just bicycled up to the gate and called, "Hey, is it all right if Tex comes in too?"

Joey was out in the yard, throwing the rolled-up hat for Eric to retrieve. If he was flabbergasted to see the visitor at his gate, he concealed it behind his gruff answer: "Sure, I guess so—if they don't fight."

Eric and Tex approached each other warily. They circled and sniffed and touched noses. The beagle, knowing he trespassed on a strange dog's home-place, rolled over on his back, paws flopping, to show how harmless his intentions were. Eric sniffed and wagged. He hunkered down on his forelegs, rear end swayed by his vigorously waving tail, and woofed at his prostrate guest.

149

"Hey, look, he wants Tex to play," said Bob.

Tex accepted the invitation. He scrambled to his feet, white-tipped tail whipping the air, and pounced on the old felt hat.

"Oh-oh," said Joey. "Eric's pretty keen on that hat."

Tex's choice obviously worried Eric. His brow furrowed in a frown. He trotted close beside the big beagle, their bodies occasionally bumping. Tex settled down to chew the soft felt. In deepening concern Eric watched him, one ear erect, one flopped over. Carefully avoiding the beagle's teeth, Eric took hold of one end of the roll and tugged gently. Tex continued to chew.

Should he rescue Eric's treasure, Joey wondered? Before he could decide, Eric changed tactics. Suddenly he showed great interest in a nearby walnut tree where squirrels often visited. Though there were none to be seen now, Eric made rushing sorties at the base of the tree, his high-pitched yips indicating a scent of highest importance.

Tex dropped the hat and charged across the yard to investigate. Quickly Eric swooped down on the felt roll and headed for the back door of the garage, always left open these days to give him a dry retreat in case of rain. The boys followed. So—after a bewildered interval of fruitless sniffing—did Tex.

In the garage was a box of Eric's possessions: his leash and comb and brush, his ball, his nylon bone with its tantalizing ham flavor, his tough rubber mouse that squeaked. Eric made straight for the box and dropped into it the old felt hat. Then with his treasure put safely away, he came cavorting and frolicking from the garage, ready once more to play with his guest.

Bob shouted with laughter. "Didja see that? Hey, wasn't that neat? . . . You stay outa there, Tex! Eric told you polite as could be that's not for you to chew up. Boy, that's a *real* smart pup!"

Anna heard the laughter and the boys' voices and came to the back door. She smiled with pleasure to see that Joey had a friend visiting him. It was lonesome for the boy here, she knew it well—not at all like the farm, where Benny and Claus and Johnny had been underfoot as constantly as her own sons. Anna had just finished scrubbing the kitchen floor, a chore that she still performed in old-country style, on hands and knees. Damp splotches stained the skirt of her work dress; her apron was hiked up around her waist; she was in stocking feet. Without thought of her appearance, she dried her soapy hands on her apron and called hospitably.

"Joey, ask your friend once, would he like some fresh raisin cookies and a cup of *appelwijn?*"

Joey's face burned hot as a stove lid over a roaring wood fire. Nobody at the House—he just knew it!—ever came to the door looking like the cleaning woman and sounding so—so Dutchy! He couldn't look at Bob. If the guy dared to laugh—if he made a single wisecrack—

But there was only enthusiasm, no mockery at all, in Bob's voice as he said, *"Appelwijn?* That's cider, isn't it? Boy, sounds great!"

Joey gave him a sidelong suspicious glance. Was this just good manners? The sort of well-bred politeness Eric had shown in putting away the treasure that was too good to be mauled?

But Bob's grin was as genuine as his voice had sounded. He looked toward the doorway with anticipatory relish. "Honest-to-goodness homemade cookies?" he said. "Not store bought? Boy, you really live it up!"

The tension eased out of Joey's shoulders; his pulsing blood cooled. Unexpectedly he laughed aloud, a big rib-stretching gusty laugh.

"You bet!" he shouted. "C'mon—let's have at it!"

Yes, it was most surprising, the changes that one furry, friendly puppy could bring about.

22

ooooooooo

FRIENDSHIP WAS too strong a term to describe the association that developed between Joey and Bob Barton that winter. Rather, it was a sort of cautious acceptance. But on Joey's part, even that much of a change was revolutionary.

It couldn't have happened, even with Eric's help, if Joey had gone on bristling with resentment at Bob's achievements. But as his own achievements increased in number, his jealousy of Bob's lessened.

Eric, of course, was his number-one achievement. Handsome, alert, every bit as regal as Joey had boasted, so quick to learn that he was the pride of the entire 4-H Club . . . yes, definitely Eric was the mainspring of Joey's new personality.

A good report card was an achievement. If there'd been such an award, Joey could have qualified by semester's end as Hopkins' Most Improved Scholar.

Being named Junior Dealer of the Month was a *big* achievement. Joey earned the title in December with the most new "starts" of any *Journal* carrier, prompt payment of his paper bill, and not one complaint from a customer.

Increasing his route had been Joey's goal since the day Eric was lost. He had to buy more fencing to make Eric's run dog-tight. More fencing meant more money, and what he was earning on his new route barely covered school expenses.

Just the thought of selling—whether *Journal* subscriptions or garden vegetables—scared Joey wordless, but his need now was too important to be throttled by shyness. So he lay awake nights, thinking of reasons why *everyone* should read the *Journal*; he practiced his sales speech while he jogged with Eric; and then—firmly, courteously, at his businesslike best—he marched himself up to every householder in his district who wasn't already a customer . . .

And sold. And sold!

Track was an achievement. By spring Joey could jog alongside Eric for as much as three miles without getting winded. He had added two inches to his chest measurements and four to his chest expansion. His showing in spring training was so satisfactory that the coach was heard to say, "The high school getting Van is likely to get the state distance championship too!" Joey, when the report reached him, didn't know which made him prouder—the coach's prediction or the name. Van. A *big* improvement over "the Kink"!

No, Joey didn't have to scowl jealously in the background anymore, or brag and fight and yell to win attention. And now that he could meet Bob Barton on practically equal terms, he found the big fellow not quite the same, somehow. That is, Bob still had all the qualities Joey had disliked—only now Joey was seeing them from a different viewpoint.

Take band, for instance.

"Hey, how come you're still in Beginners Band?" Bob asked one winter Saturday when he and Tex joined Joey and Eric for a hike. "Y'oughta get moved up to Intermediate. Lot more fun." That was the bossy Bob, the lordly know-it-all, talking.

"Huh!" snorted Joey. "Only place Mr. Frank'd move *me* is out!"

"Aw, he's not such a bad guy. Whyn't you talk to him about it?" (Apple polisher, teacher's pet—that's who was speaking then.)

"Are you kiddin'?"

"Heck, no. I'll go with you, if you want. How about Monday after school?" (A pushy, shoving apple polisher now; but when it was Joey's cause that he forwarded, how oddly that changed things!)

"For Pete's sake!" muttered Joey in extreme discomfort.

Nor did Bob forget a project once it was launched. It would be easier to halt a glacier, Joey discovered, than stand in the way of Bob's good will. Monday afternoon, red-eared with embarrassment, Joey found himself irresistibly propelled into Mr. Frank's office.

"Move Joey up? Sure thing," said Mr. Frank. "As soon as he learns that a drumstick isn't a croquet mallet, and the object of drumming isn't to split the drumskin."

Joey looked longingly toward the door, measuring the seconds it would take him to escape.

Bob wasn't at all discouraged. "How about if he practices real hard—I mean an awful lot?"

Joey mumbled hastily, "Don' have a drum."

"You don't need one," said Mr. Frank. "Take along a pair of drumsticks; you can practice on anything—desk, table, your mother's ironing board. Here, let's see how you hold the sticks. . . ."

It was ghastly, especially with Bob hanging over his shoulder, but somehow Joey managed to give Mr. Frank's desk a whack or two.

Mr. Frank winced as though he, instead of the desk, had been Joey's target. "Let's take it from the beginning again," he said patiently. "Right hand— palm flat—hold the stick with your thumb; that's it. Left hand shakes hands with the stick. Start with taps—four right, four left. Now a paradiddle; right, left, right, right—left, right, left, left. . . . Let's get a beat into it: *right*, left, right—*left*, right, left—*keep* it up—"

Joey could feel Bob's breath on his cheek. He concentrated terribly hard, tongue between teeth, mind shutting out every thought, every sound but the steady beat emphasized by Mr. Frank's voice.

"*Once* again—*keep* it up—*once* again—fine, fine!"

Joey was so startled he bit his tongue. Bob whacked him on the shoulder, "See? I knew you could do it! He'll be ready for Intermediate in no time, won't he, Mr. Frank?"

Mr. Frank made a valiant, if hopeless, effort to resist the glacier. "We'll see," he said.

From then on Bob brought not only Tex but his clarinet along when he came to Joey's house. "Thought maybe we'd get in some practicing," he'd say, as though there were any "maybe" about it!

Before the new year was a month old, Joey had joined Bob in Intermediate and was practicing even more diligently. Now he not only had to keep up with more skilled performers; he had to meet the standards of Advanced Band by school year's end. At least that's what Bob *said* they were both going to do, and by now Joey pretty well knew what that meant. The glacier was on the move again.

Yes, Bob was still all the things Joey had grumbled about. And he still lived in the spreading, well-manicured, impressive House—though it was surprising how amiably at home he could make himself in Anna's kitchen! And he still bragged up Tex as though no finer beagle had ever bayed on a rabbit's trail.

But then again (Joey had to admit) he praised Eric with equal enthusiasm. How could you stay sore at a guy like that? Just goofy about dogs, that's what he was, whether the dog was his own or somebody else's! Joey wondered how that could be; for him, taking pride in a dog went along with pride in owning the dog (in his innermost mind, Eric was already—in fact, had always been—his).

So the truce continued as gray wintry rainy days gave way to an early sweet-flowering spring such as Joey had never seen before. Every yard blossomed like an Easter bonnet with lacy yellows and lavenders and flaming corals; every country road was lined with puffs of pink and white.

"Chee, back home they're still havin' *blizzards!*" Joey reminded himself, dazzled by the colorful profusion.

Bob's weekend plans grew more ambitious. "Why don't we hike out to the coast some Saturday? Look for agates 'n' shells an' those glass floats—you ever seen 'em? Japanese fishermen use 'em on their lines; sometimes they break loose 'n' float clear across the Pacific. We could start out real early, soon as I finish my route . . . "

"Huh-uh," said Joey. "We couldn't get back in time for *my* route."

"Hey, that's right, you're still delivering *Journal*s. How come there hasn't been a *Star* vacancy? You checked with Mr. Hammond lately?"

"I don't want—" Joey began.

But the glacier, implacably rolling ahead, crunched his words into small pebbles. "How about if *I* talk to him too? I bet he'd find something pretty quick if we both kept after him."

"I don't want a *Star* route," Joey said more loudly.

" 'Course you do. More money in it, get it over with early in the morning. Only the new kids get stuck with the *Journal*." Bob had good qualities, but tact wasn't one of them. Now, all unthinking, he had blundered into an especially sensitive area.

"I'm NOT stuck with the *Journal!*" Joey said, very loudly indeed. "I LIKE the *Journal!* Best paper in Westport!"

"Well, sure . . ." The glacier was momentarily slowed by Joey's vehemence. "It's the *only* paper in Westport."

"That's what I MEAN. That's why it's IMPOR-TANT. How much local news d'you get outa the

Star? EVERYBODY in Westport oughta take the *Journal!*" It surprised Joey to realize how much of his December sales speech he still remembered. It surprised him still more to find he'd sold not only his customers on the *Journal* but himself, too. " 'Cause the *Journal*'s YOUR paper!" he added.

"Well, all *right!*" The glacier ground to a stop. "You don't hafta yell," Bob said mildly. "I hear ya." He reconsidered Saturday's plan and suggested, "How about if we take pack-lunches and hike up the butte? Tex is crazy about the butte. Way he acts, you'd think he smelled a mountain lion!"

"Huh, he better stick to rabbits!" Joey scoffed, but not as tartly as he might have. Making fun of Bob's beagle was now only the shadow of an old habit. In fact, if pressed, Joey would have had to admit his sneaking affection for the old dog. "Okay. Eight o'clock?"

"Earlier! Weather like this, the whole town could be picnicking there by afternoon. How about seven?"

The glacier had recovered from shock and was rolling again, but now its force didn't dismay Joey. He'd stopped it once; he could do it again.

"Okay," he agreed. "Eric 'n' me'll be ready."

For anything (he almost added). Even a mountain lion. Even a glacier.

160

23

○○○○○○○○○

THE BUTTE ON the edge of town was a favorite climbing spot for Westport's young people. The sturdiest climbers chose the steeper, more heavily wooded north side; the less athletic clambered up the gently sloping south side; those who wanted the view from the top with the least expense of energy hiked or rode up the bridle trail that circled upward from the little park at the butte's south base.

Later in the day the park would be alive with fluttering dots of children. Schools held their picnics there and families their reunions. Always there were children climbing over the concrete animals in the playground, riding the real ponies in the sawdust circle, pressing awed faces against the barrier that separated them from the monkey house, the screened bird shelters, the den in which two small brown bears paced restlessly.

But when Joey and Bob crossed the park, it was eerily quiet, still wrapped in early-morning mists. Tex growled deep in his throat; the fur on Eric's neck rose in a dark ridge.

"Hey, hold it; aren't any mountain lions in the

park, for Pete's sake!" Bob said. He asked Joey, "How about it—want to try the north side?"

"Sure," Joey agreed.

Straight up the steep slope they scrabbled, higher and higher, grabbing at bushes and saplings for handholds. The dogs, zigzagging to take advantage of every natural path, were soon out of sight, their progress marked by Eric's excited barks and the beagle's fluting *Ah-oooooo!*

The boys stopped a moment to get ther breaths and listen. "Sounds like they've found the bridle trail," said Bob as the mingled barks and bays neared and faded on a horizontal line above them. "The sissies are takin' the easy way up."

"Or else they're following a pretty smart mountain lion," panted Joey, scrambling to a higher level on hands and knees. "Only a *dumb* cat would take this trail."

"You tryin' to tell me something?" Bob grinned, humping after him. "C'mon, you prairie dog, *I'll* show you how to climb!" He surged ahead of Joey, lost his footing and went skidding, bumping, bouncing downward till he came up against a tree.

Above him, Joey hooked his arm around a sapling and shouted with laughter. "Like that, huh? Think I'll jus' stick to prairie-doggin'!"

Bob wasn't laughing. His intent expression silenced Joey. "Listen!"

"It's just the dogs," said Joey. The duet, quite distant now, thrilled on a new note of excitement. "Sounds like maybe they treed somethin'."

But Bob wasn't listening to the dogs. "It's from down in the park," he said. "What d'ya suppose happened?"

And now Joey, too, could hear blurred shouts, mingled voices, the wail of an approaching siren. What a time to be halfway up a hill! "Hey, let's go down!"

Bob swarmed past him, scrabbling from bush to tree root to hummock of grass. "Quicker to go up! Soon as we hit that trail, we can follow it down."

Belatedly Joey remembered his responsibility for the young dog roaming somewhere above him. "Maybe I better get Eric first."

"Aw, he's okay. He'll follow Tex down."

Joey wasn't so sure. The excited pitch of the dogs' barking contributed to his uneasiness. What if they *had* treed something—something dangerous? "Hey, you were kiddin', weren't you? 'Bout mountain lions on the butte?"

Bob didn't hear him. Scuttling like a reckless crab, he plunged through a screen of bushes and yelled back, "Here's the trail! C'mon!" His pounding footsteps faded as he raced down the bridle path.

Joey, when he reached the trail, hesitated only a moment before following him. The sounds from the park were more exciting than the racket the dogs were making. When the boys rounded the curve of the trail, they saw an ambulance and several police cars in the park below them. While they watched, a car with the state seal on its door swung in beside the others. The park caretaker ran toward it, gesturing wildly. A man jumped out of the car, then from the back seat carefully removed a gun.

"Chee!" Joey said in awe. "What's goin' *on?"*

"Big robbery downtown!" Bob guessed. "They got the criminals cornered in the monkey house!"

A police officer glanced upward, spotted the boys on the butte, and made a sweeping motion to come down. Through cupped hands he reinforced the order with a shout. "You two up there! Get down here right away!"

"What'd *we* do?" Joey asked Bob in bewilderment.

"Search me! No law against climbin' the butte—is there?"

Others in the park were yelling and gesturing at the pair. "Hustle!" roared the police officer.

Thoroughly alarmed now, the two boys went skidding and slipping down the slope. *"We* didn't do

164

nothin'," they protested in unison, with a worried look at the man with the gun.

The officer was scanning the butte. "Any more of you up there?"

"N-no," said Joey, "only—"

"Stay right here," the officer directed, "till we round up the bear."

"The—huh?" Bob croaked.

"Or at least find out where he is." The officer strode off to join the man with the gun.

Bob tried to stop the caretaker as he hurried past. "What happened?"

"Vandals!" The park caretaker looked a little wild-eyed; his fluff of white hair stirred in the breeze he created. "Vagrants! Juvenile delinquents!"

A bystander contributed more information. "Some joker smashed the lock on the bear cage last night. Must've had a car to get away in."

Joey wondered what was funny about letting bears loose. He looked nervously toward the ambulance. "Who—who got hurt?"

"Nobody. Yet. They collared one bear over at the picnic tables; the garbage can looked better to that fellow than freedom. But the other bear just up and disappeared."

"When they find it"—the same idea was in both boys' minds; they looked from each other to the man with the gun—"do they . . . will they have to shoot it?"

"Just put it to sleep," the bystander assured them. "That thing shoots tranquilizing darts. They sent right off to the state zoo for it, soon as they found the bears were out."

Joey felt better about waiting to see the end of the hunt. A bear on the loose was dangerous, of course; but a bear he'd watched and enjoyed every time he went through the park—well, that made it different. More like a pet. Like a big shaggy brown dog—

"*Dog!*" squawked Joey. He plunged for the trail leading up the butte. Bob gave a strangled yelp and followed.

"Come back here!" the police officer shouted. "You boys, stay off the butte!"

Footsteps thudded after them. Joey gave an anguished glance back over his shoulder. "Our dogs!" he yelled. "That's what they been barkin' at. They got the bear up there—" *Or the bear's got them!* The thought doubled his speed.

Even so, the officer overtook him. He stopped the boys with a powerful hand on each shoulder.

"You don't *understand!*" cried Joey, struggling to get free. "Eric's up there—"

"You lemme go!" Bob roared. "I gotta get Tex!"

"You'll get your dogs," the officer promised. "Just stay behind us!"

He and the man with the gun took the lead and put ground behind them at a pace Mr. Dedham would have admired. So would Joey ordinarily. Right now he had room for only one thought: Eric was up there on the thickly wooded hillside. Eric—and a bear.

Now, distantly, he could once more hear barking. Barking—or baying? *Both!* Joey's heart leaped with relief, then was pinched with new fright at the shrill thin sound of Eric's barks, the hoarseness of Tex's *Ah-oooooo!* A puppy and an old worn-out dog, that's all they were. A puppy and a tired old dog—and a bear.

Even by the easy-rising path, it seemed to take endless hours to climb the butte. Joey's heart hammered in his ears; he breathed with pain. *Slow down,* Mr. Dedham would have told him; *you're not running the fifty-yard dash; pace yourself.* But Joey wasn't racing now for the glory of Hopkins and Joey Van Oolbekink; he was running to Eric's aid. Thought of the dog in trouble blotted every concern from his mind but the necessity to keep his stumbling heavy feet moving.

So concentrated was he on putting one foot ahead of the other that he ran smack into the police officer's backstretched warning arm. "Hold it!" said the officer. "They're coming this way!"

"Get off the path—behind the trees, all of you!" The man with the gun cocked it and eased quietly behind a screen of bushes.

Joey would rather have rushed on. Now that he could hear something besides the pound-pound of the blood in his ears, he knew the dogs were very close. The pitch of Eric's barking sounded frantic. *Idjit, why don't you just cut and RUN?* he begged the dog silently. *You could get away safe—you could get here to us!* If he could just whistle him to come . . .

But from behind his screen of greenery the man with the gun was cautioning them to be absolutely quiet. Joey could only freeze behind his tree. And wait and hope and—

Here they came! The bear—no, the dogs—no— which was chasing which? In his excitement Joey almost forgot orders and popped into sight. *Nobody* was being chased! The dogs were *herding* the bear down the trail! Anyway, Eric was herding, for all the world like the shepherd dogs on the farm back home. Tex was puffing in the rear, cutting off the bear's retreat with his hoarse warnings. But Eric was everywhere— now on this side, now darting to the other as the bear turned that way—deftly, skillfully keeping the confused and harassed and tiring beast on the trail.

The man raised his gun. "Don't!" cried Joey impulsively. But the shot had already zinged home. The bear roared. He swung to face this new enemy, reared up fearsomely on his hind legs, clawed the air with a mighty swipe of deadly paws . . .

And sank to the ground.

"Why'd you do that?" Joey protested. "Eric was bringing him in jus' fine—oh, Eric, Eric, you dumb good dog, you! Herding *bears*, for Pete's sake!" On his knees beside the panting, grinning, excited dog, Joey demanded again, "Whyn't you let Eric finish the job? He was doin' *great!*"

"That he was," agreed the man with the gun. "But I couldn't take the chance. You wouldn't have been so happy if the bear had taken a swipe at him with those claws."

"Aw, Eric could've stayed out of reach—he's *fast!*" Joey boasted. Suddenly the sum total of the last hour's terror and excitement and physical strain hit him. He couldn't have gotten to his feet, not even if the bear had wakened and charged him! "Gee," he said weakly, "I guess you're right. Maybe Eric could've lasted till he got him down—but not me!"

Bob had been trying to coax Tex away from the bear. Finally he picked the dog up and came staggering down the trail with his squirming burden. "Golly, Tex has gone *nuts!* I s'pose now he thinks he's a big-game hunter!"

The man with the gun said, "We'd better bring up the gear and get this fellow home before he wakes up." The police officer and the stragglers just now catching up with the chase turned back down the trail. With a last awed look at the fallen hero of this morning's adventure, the boys followed.

At the foot of the butte Bob dropped Tex and wriggled his aching shoulders. "Let's eat, huh?"

"Here?" Joey looked around the park in vague surprise. Food at a picnic table seemed an oddly tame ending to a safari like theirs. He said, "We never did get to the top of the butte."

"Well, we went halfway up twice; that took just as much muscle . . . *Hey, Tex!* Drat that crazy dog!" The beagle, as soon as he was released, had started again up the trail. Bob retrieved him. This time he made a leash of his belt and anchored the dog to the picnic table. Tex refused the bite of sandwich Bob offered him. Sagging against the leg of the table, limp with weariness, tongue lolling out almost full length, the beagle stared with glazed eyes at the butte and dreamed of more bears to conquer. Bob said, "I bet if a rabbit crossed the park right this minute, Tex'd just sneer at it! Prob'ly won't chase anything smaller'n a cow after today." He stroked the old dog fondly. "Boy, think you're some hunter, don't ya?"

Eric lay quietly at Joey's side, as he'd been told to do. From time to time Joey glanced down at the smooth dark head, the alert ears tipped forward to catch every word. Joey's heart swelled with pride . . .

And something else. Something that had nothing to do with the glory of Eric's performance on the butte and the reflected glow it cast on Joey. Something more like—love.

Joey took a bite of sandwich and couldn't swallow it. The swelling had reached his throat. *Chee, was he gonna bawl, for Pete's sake?* Hastily, he bent over to pat Eric and praise him with a gruff, "Good ol' dog!"

"Gee, yeh, he certainly is!" Bob agreed generously. He bit into his own sandwich and, while he chewed, stared at the butte as bemusedly as Tex. "Boy, it's sure a shame you can't keep him!"

IV

ooooooooo

End and
Beginning

24

OOOOOOOOO

THE WORDS FELL like cold, hard stones. Joey felt each separate painful impact. *A shame you can't keep him. Can't keep him. Can't keep him.*

They were bringing the bear down on a sort of flat sleigh. "Hey, let's go watch!" cried Bob. He unleashed Tex and rushed across the park.

Joey didn't follow. "Eric, heel," he said automatically and plodded toward Orchard Lane. Obediently the half-grown dog trotted close at his left side. From time to time he looked up anxiously into Joey's face and whined. "What's wrong?" he asked dog fashion, but there was no answer to his question, no reassuring pat on his upraised head.

Can't keep him. The echo kept pace with Joey's feet. *Can't keep him.*

It was something he'd forgotten, something he had chosen not to remember. *Can't keep him.* In the beginning it hadn't mattered. Eric was something to be shown off with pride—a prized possession, something of Joey's own to set against Bob Barton's lavish total. If not Eric, another dog would do.

But Eric had become—Eric. Heart-close friend and companion.

Can't keep him.

Joey's unregarded feet carried him to the gate on Orchard Lane. He looked at it in faint surprise, opened it, let Eric into his run, walked blindly through the kitchen.

"*Ach*, you're home!" Anna greeted him, with a smile. "Did you have a good climb? Was there food enough?"

Joey didn't answer. He didn't even know she'd spoken. He went upstairs to his room and shut the door and sat on the bed.

Can't keep him.

"I *gotta* keep him!" *Eric and me, we'll start out for Iowa . . .* the words had the familiarity of an old record. When had he said them before?

No use; they'd track him down, the people who owned Eric. He was too valuable to be allowed to disappear without an outcry and search. Hadn't Mr. Sanford answered Joey's hinting questions, months ago, with the flat statement that no, they'd never sell Eric to him? Then certainly they wouldn't just let him slip away. They'd follow him and bring him back. . . .

Can't keep him. Can't keep him.

"Joey!" called Pa. "What're you doing up there? There's work to be done."

Joey stared at the opposite wall. There had to be some way. *Some* way.

Dirk stumped up the stairs and banged on the door. He opened it and frowned at the silent boy. "Your ma wants things from the store. *I've* had no time to go, what with the ground to get ready for new planting and nobody to help me."

Most of his meaning was lost on Joey, who stared at him as at a stranger. "I'll go," he offered at last.

Dirk opened his mouth and shut it again. "Indeed!" he grunted. "Anna will take it most kindly." The tone of his voice went as unnoticed as his words. He raised and dropped his hands in a helpless gesture and clumped down the stairs. "Moonstruck," he told Anna briefly.

Joey went to the store for Anna. He picked up his bundle of *Journal*s and delivered them with automatic precision. He took Eric for his evening run and played fetch with the old felt hat. He fed the dog, ate his own supper, and went to his room.

And all the while he saw nothing, heard nothing, tasted nothing. *Can't keep him*—the shocking echo reverberated in the most secret recess of his mind. *Can't keep him*. Why, that couldn't be! His whole future was bound up in Eric. It was because of Eric that he had set his secret heart on becoming a vet, a dream so big and momentous he hadn't even phrased it in unspoken words, lest he let them slip out.

The material from the Guide Dog people, well worn with much rereading, had long since been shoved to the back of his study-table drawer. Now Joey got it out again. He sat reading it with the intensity of a man lost in the wilderness studying a map for some clue to survival. The familiar directions for Eric's care were no different than when he had so faithfully learned them last October.

"At about one year of age the puppy you have raised will go back to Guide Dogs for the Blind." Joey had reached the last page of the manual; these were the words he had skimmed through hastily, unseeingly, with very little interest. Back then, the date of Eric's eventual departure had seemed as distant, as unreal, as Joey's own adulthood. Back then, Eric had been only a handsome puppy who would help prove to all those kids at Hopkins that Joey was Somebody.

"The reason we cannot tell you exactly how long it will be from the time your puppy comes back to Guide Dogs until it will graduate is that we never know." Automatically Joey's eyes had continued to read the page and transmit the words to his mind. "Even after he has completed his training, he may not be suited to the personality of any member of the class of blind who come in for training and so may have to wait over for a later class. . . ."

On and on. More words, all dealing with an impossibility, all assuming that he could let Eric go.

"Usually your puppy will graduate within five months after it returns. . . .

"If a puppy fails in training, we notify you at once and ask if you wish to have it returned as your own dog."

Your own dog.

The dull echo of Bob's words was obliterated. The automaton was replaced by a living, breathing, wide-awake boy. *Your own dog!* Intently Joey reread the paragraph. "If a puppy fails in training . . ."

He had found the clue he was looking for.

25

○○○○○○○○○

JOEY WAS SUDDENLY and enormously hungry. When he brought Eric in for the night, he stopped at the refrigerator to see what Anna had in the way of leftovers. Mmmmm . . . sausage and pudding and cottage cheese. A fresh brown loaf of pumpernickel in the breadbox. Gingersnaps in the cookie jar. Joey constructed a towering snack and took it up to his room.

Eric, following him, went immediately to his bed. Automatically Joey started to snap the light chain to his collar ring . . .

And then let it drop. He sat down at his study table to eat, glancing from time to time at Eric, who had snuggled into a furry ball and was already asleep.

"Here, boy!" Joey woke the dog abruptly. He tossed a bit of sausage on the floor. "Come get it!"

Eric's ears tilted forward, his brow wrinkled as it always did when he was puzzled. Slowly he left his bed and advanced toward the scrap of meat. He sniffed it, drew back, and sat looking from it to Joey. Trained not to expect tidbits from the dining table, Eric was waiting politely for Joey to retrieve the fallen morsel.

180

"It's okay. Eat it. It's yours," Joey urged him. But he had to pick up the meat and hold it out to Eric before the dog would take it.

The taste was strange to Eric; he wasn't used to highly seasoned food. When Joey offered a second bite, Eric refused it and went back to his box.

Joey put on pajamas and got into bed. Softly he called, "C'mon, fellow! Come sleep up here." He patted the quilt invitingly. Eric stirred restlessly; he got up and turned around three times in the box, scratching his mat into a rumpled nest before settling down again.

"Aw, c'mon!" Joey coaxed. Eric gave a quivering sigh—and stayed where he was. Joey turned off the light and pulled the covers over him. His sigh, as he drifted into sleep, sounded very much like Eric's.

Out of habit Joey woke before the alarm sounded and shut it off. Then deliberately he snuggled back down in bed and closed his eyes. No need for hurry. It was Sunday. Of course on Sunday he had to deliver his *Journal*s in the morning, but not necessarily this early in the morning. Joey yawned luxuriously—

And was answered by a soft whine. Eric pawed at his arm and whined again.

"Go ahead an' use your papers," Joey mumbled. He pulled the covers over his head.

Eric pad-padded to the door and scratched it. He stood on his hind legs and nosed the knob. When that failed to open the door, he barked.

"Shuddup!" muttered Joey from beneath the covers.

"Rrrowf!" Eric insisted.

From across the hall Dirk rumbled, "Joey, are you awake? The dog wants out!"

"Yuck!" grumbled Joey. In pajamas and bare feet, he loped downstairs and let Eric out through the garage into his run. Back in his room again, he looked consideringly at the tumbled bed. No use returning to it. In a few minutes Eric would be barking for his breakfast. And then he'd be expecting his morning workout—and letting the whole neighborhood know of his disappointment if Joey omitted it.

Already there was a questioning yip from the back yard. "Okay, okay. I'm comin'!" Joey called from his window as he hustled into his clothes. "Just wait till it isn't Sunday," he told himself. Neighbors could get particularly grouchy about being wakened early on a Sunday morning, but weekdays were different. Weekdays he'd just let Eric bark till the pup got over the idea that a day's happenings marched along with the regularity of a drumbeat.

"Don't be sore," he whispered, hugging the dog hard for a moment as he set his breakfast on the floor.

"We *gotta* do it this way, see? Or else—"

No, he wouldn't think beyond "or else." There just wasn't going to be any "or else"!

Anna could not understand why suddenly Joey lost interest in his daily workouts with Eric. "The poor doggy!" she protested. "All day he waits for you to come and take him for his run."

"Haven't time," Joey said hastily. "Gotta theme to write. Hey, will you give him his supper?" Anna stared after the boy in open-mouthed amazement.

"That dog of yours!" Dirk grumbled. "He stands at his fence with that hat in his mouth and whines at me!"

"Whyn't you throw it for him a couple of times?" Joey suggested.

"*Me* throw it?" Dirk echoed in surprise. "And if I say 'let go' instead of 'drop it,' the world will not end, no?"

"Aw, Eric'll know what you mean." Joey escaped quickly before Dirk's questions could grow more penetrating.

Bob too was puzzled by the change in Joey's attitude.

"C'mon, boy, let's get goin'." Joey snapped his fingers at Eric as he and Bob and Tex started on their next Saturday hike.

"That's funny," said Bob.

183

"What's funny?"

"That's the first time you didn't say, 'Eric—heel.' "

"So what? You think he's dumb or somethin'? He understands all right."

"Yeh, but—I thought you *had* to—" Bob watched Eric step along smartly at Joey's left side, just as usual, in spite of the sloppy way Joey was letting the leash drag. "Oh, well, skip it. You got him trained so good now, I guess he'd do the right thing even if you just wiggled your ears."

"That's not so!" Joey's voice bristled with fierce indignation. His cheeks burned; his eyes sparked with what Bob took for anger but which could have been moisture. "Don't you dare say that!"

"What'd I say?" Bob asked helplessly. "Good grief, a guy can't say boo anymore 'thout you blowin' your top."

The hike wasn't too successful. Joey appeared to be in a contrary mood. Repeatedly he teased Eric, till Bob protested, "Hey, you're gonna make him bite you if you rough him up like that."

"Aw, Eric wouldn't bite, would you, boy?" Again Joey grabbed the dog and wrestled him to the ground. And again Eric got to his feet and patiently returned to his place at Joey's side. "You dumb fool, you!" Joey burst out, and this time the anger—or the tears?—was in his voice. "Let's go home," he said abruptly, and without waiting for Bob's answer, marched off.

The following weekend Bob didn't suggest a hike. Nor did Joey.

The season for leisurely Saturdays was over in any case, for now the day brought track meets with other junior high schools. Joey was a member of the distance relay team, running third position, and he competed also in the two-twenty-yard dash. Coach Dedham, knowing he had a winner in long-distance events, tried to promote a cross-country event but without success.

"Looks like you'll have to wait till high school to show your mettle," the coach admitted. "But don't worry, the time will come. Keep up your workouts. Let's see, you're the one who jogs with your dog, aren't you?"

"Yeh," said Joey. "I mean—yessir."

"Fine, fine. A dog makes a great jogging partner. Keep it up."

"Yeh," said Joey. Mr. Dedham wondered at the boy's suddenly bleak expression.

Mr. Sanford met Joey at the entrance of Hopkins. "Well, Joey, not too long now till Eric goes back, is it? I suppose you want to enter him in the 4-H Fair next week."

"No," said Joey.

"You *don't?*" Mr. Sanford was genuinely surprised. "It's just about your last chance to show him off."

"He's not ready," Joey muttered. "Got a lot of bad habits, have to be worked out."

"*Eric?*" Mr. Sanford couldn't believe his ears.

"Yeh." Joey plunged on hurriedly, "I bet he'll never make a good Guide Dog. Prob'ly all my fault."

"Why, Joey, you've done a *splendid* job with Eric! I'm sure the people at San Rafael are going to be very happy with him when he goes back."

Joey gave him such a stricken look, before he turned and ran down the steps, that the 4-H director was shaken; what could he possibly have said to so offend the boy?

Slowly Joey pedaled toward Orchard Lane. Homecoming now was the most depressing hour of the day; Joey postponed it as long as he could. Once he had whizzed through the quiet streets, eager for his first glimpse of house and yard—and the black nose thrust between pickets in joyous welcome.

But now going home meant only a sullen time of deliberately neglected duties. Omitting the daily rehearsal of Eric's commands. Ignoring the old felt hat when Eric dropped it hopefully at his feet. Letting Anna feed the dog, and not even checking up on how

186

many forbidden leftovers found their way into his bowl. Hardest of all, leaving Eric behind, whining at the fence, when he went jogging. Joey didn't think it safe to let Eric run with him now; what if he gave him an order—*stop, sit, heel*—when they reached a busy intersection, and Eric didn't obey? No, he couldn't take the chance.

Glumly Joey pushed his bike through the gate. Eric leaped against the wire fencing, woof-woofing in high excitement. He ran into the garage and brought out the old felt hat. "*Rrruff!*" he barked as he dropped it expectantly.

"Well, jus' once," Joey relented. He leaned over the wire, scooped up the hat, and threw it to the end of the run. Delightedly the young dog rushed after it; when he returned, Joey was just disappearing into the house.

Eric's wagging tail slowed and drooped. Intently he watched the door for his master's return. When Joey appeared again, his school clothes exchanged for sweater and jeans and tennis shoes, Eric bounded against the wire in great leaps that made the posts quiver.

"Throttle down," Joey told him. "You gotta stay home."

Eric's barks grew piercing. Giving up his attack on the fence, he charged into the garage and came out dragging something that whipped around his legs and almost tripped him up. "*Arrr, arrr, arrr!*" he whined in such anxiety that Joey, his hand on the gate, was forced to stop and look back.

The dog stood on his hind legs, big forepaws pressed against the wire, a length of leash trailing from his jaws. "*Arrr, arrrrr!*" he begged.

"Aw, *Eric!*" cried Joey. Suddenly he was across the yard and kneeling at the fence, his hands reaching through the wire to grab double handfuls of thick fur. Tears too long dammed inside him poured down his cheeks. He repeated helplessly, "Aw, *Eric*—why d'ya have to be such a *good* dog?"

Eric's cold nose pushed against the wire to nuzzle the boy. His long rough tongue came out and licked away the tears as fast as they fell. Deep in his throat he made small rumbling sounds of comfort.

Joey swallowed more tears. He gulped, "What'm I gonna *do* about you?" But the words held not so much despair as sad acceptance. Eric's comfort had taken the keen edge from his anguish. His tears slowed; his breath caught on a ragged sigh; his grip on the dog's fur loosened.

Eric, quick to sense the change of mood, responded happily. He licked the last taste of salt from Joey's cheeks, then again caught up the leash and jingled it. "*Rowf!*" he urged.

Joey gave a shaky little laugh. He smoothed the furrow between the dog's bright questioning dark eyes. "Okay, boy," he said. "You win."

Eric's excitement was tremendous as Joey let him out of the run. He leaped and pranced and dashed helter-skelter at tree and bush and boy.

"Enough of that," Joey told him gruffly. "We're playing it your way, remember?" He snapped the leash to the dog's collar. For just a moment more he held back; then the words came clearly and firmly.

"Eric—heel!"

26

ooooooooo

JOEY TOOK a sort of melancholy pride in Eric's stubborn refusal to lapse into bad habits.

"That's a real smart dog," he told Anna and Dirk and Bob and Mr. Sanford and every classmate at Hopkins. Just as though it was a brand-new quality he'd just discovered. Just as though Eric hadn't proved how smart he was over and over again during his months in Westport, until everyone was already in complete agreement with Joey's statement. "Teach him something an' he stays taught!"

To nobody did Joey explain why he had tried to unteach Eric during those unhappy weeks. Anna blamed it on the pressure of school work; the boy was trying too hard to finish the year with top-lofty grades that would make up for his poor start. And as for all that running!—Anna didn't care how many trophies Hopkins had added to its collection this spring; it was asking too much of a growing boy to so tire himself he hadn't energy left to feed his own dog!

Bob didn't puzzle his head over possible explanations of Joey's abruptly changed attitude. If asked, he would have said vaguely, "Oh, I dunno—he's kinda funny sometimes. Like last fall—boy, that kid had a chip on his shoulder bigger'n a Douglas fir! Always sore about somethin'—*I* don't know what."

Dirk had his own ideas, but he kept them to himself. He had been a boy once—hard as it was for Joey to imagine it—and he recognized a boy's buttoned-up grief when he saw it. *"Yah*, now comes the hard time," he nodded in silent sympathy. "Growing up, it's not all cocoa and honeycakes!"

Weekend hikes were resumed. To the dogs' delight, the sunny but cool May Sundays were spent in the hills or on a leisurely trek upriver. It was good to walk and jog himself tired, Joey found, so that when the foursome stopped to rest, he had no thought beyond catching his breath.

"Lots of places we gotta go yet," Bob said one Sunday as they lay on their stomachs and watched the river current curl and froth around the rocks, " 'fore Eric—" With unusual tact, he didn't finish the sentence. "You know what? We oughta get to the top of that butte just once, anyway, 'fore—hey, why don't we go there the very last Sunday 'fore—"

There was no way to avoid the word. Every plan, every thought, every sentence led to it. Bob heaved a mighty sigh. Tact and sensitivity were not second nature to him; learning to think before he spoke was proving a difficult lesson.

"—'fore school lets out," he finished gamely. No date had been established for Eric's departure, but both boys took for granted it would coincide with the end of school.

"Yeh," Joey agreed. He sensed the effort Bob was making and, in gratitude, tried to inject heartiness into his answer. "Yeh, let's do that!"

They had made so many plans for the last days. *Let's do that; haven't ever done that; got to do this one more time.* In an odd way the pleasant, bright-flowering spring season seemed to Joey more like fall; there was the same mixture of sadness in its enjoyment that he felt in Indian summer with its brilliant colors and hazy blue skies and smell of bonfires.

Maybe because Indian summer, too, betokened an ending.

And yet—every year Joey had a vague, secret, ridiculous hope that *this* year Indian summer might go on and on and on. Till Christmas, maybe. Possibly even till spring.

Now the same unspoken hope sustained him. Maybe—just maybe—some miracle would yet occur. If he walked the length of this railing without falling . . . if he bicycled all the way from home to Hopkins without having to stop for a red light . . . if he got an A in science . . . if he paid back every penny he'd taken from those lockers last fall . . .

The amounts were still penciled in the back of his notebook, reminding him that he had always considered them "loans." He could afford to pay them back now; his burgeoning paper route brought in more than his expenses; he had even been giving Dirk money to put in the savings account, his old sense of injury at the lost bank book mollified by time and the winter's great satisfactions. Really all that stood in the way of repayment now was—how to do it? The desperation that had made him take risk after risk in October was absent now.

Until it reappeared in the desperate need for a miracle.

Joey considered the largest amount—sixty-four cents from locker 121. A kid who left that much change lying around in an open locker and didn't report its loss might very well *never* turn a lock on his possessions. Joey carried the exact change in his pocket for two days, waiting for a moment when the hall was empty . . .

Then swiftly tried the door. Once again it swung open. Joey's heart lurched much faster than when theft had been his motive. Swiftly he dumped his handful of change on the locker shelf and quietly closed the door. Nobody had seen him; he was safe. Weak with relief, he slipped into a classroom.

Okay, he told himself, *okay. Now if you can get*

the rest of it back, maybe—maybe—

He found other lockers open. A dime here, a nickel here, fifteen cents there, one by one his debts were paid. He'd been right; a student who didn't bother to lock his locker one time might very well forget it another. But a final repayment plagued him; one locker was never open and time was getting short. Daringly Joey hovered nearby till he saw its owner pause to exchange books for another class, then ran after him, calling, "Hey, you dropped this!" The boy looked in surprise at the dime Joey thrust on him, then shrugged and pocketed it.

I did it! Joey said exultantly. *Now maybe— maybe—*

Little more than a week of school remained when curiosity halted Joey at locker 297. Still frighteningly clear in his mind were the terrifying minutes when he hadn't been able to get rid of that purse with its damning roll of bills. Who was the girl? Was she always that careless?

Tentatively Joey tried the handle of the locker as he passed. The door remained tight-closed.

"Hey, what're you doing?" a voice asked suspiciously.

Joey's heart hammered. He hesitated a moment between flight and brazen encounter, then swung around.

"Jus' checkin'," he said casually. The appearance of the big girl by the locker surprised him. He had expected someone—well, someone Bob Bartonish Well-dressed. A look of casual plenty. But even to his inexperienced eyes, it was obvious that the girl's cotton dress was faded from much washing and her sweater had been outgrown months before. "You left a wad a' bills in your locker once, with the door open. I locked it."

"Hah!" scoffed the girl. "Me?"

"Well, you did," Joey said defensively. " 'Cause I looked in your purse an' saw them, so there! You're jus' lucky I didn't decide to keep it!"

He was shocked to hear himself making such an admission, but the girl's disbelief had nettled him. Now her expression changed. She looked sober, almost scared.

"Oh, *that* day," she said. "Honest, did I leave the locker open? Oh, migosh!"

Joey looked at her curiously, his own alarm forgotten in her obvious shock. Her eyes had widened, her cheeks had lost their high color. "Golly!" she murmured. "That could've been bad." She added in explanation, "It wasn't my money. It was our club dues. I'm treasurer."

She looked so shaken that Joey felt compelled to reassure her. "Oh, well, you'd have got it back, even if somebody *had* swiped it. They'd have caught the thief." Remembering his panic that *he'd* be the one they caught before he could replace the money, Joey shivered.

The big girl didn't notice. Her attention was still directed inward at the specter that had frightened her. "You don't understand," she said. "You see"—impulsively she let the specter loose, banishing it by exposure to the light of day—"they'd never have believed it was really swiped. By anyone but me."

"*Who* wouldn't?"

"Well—my folks, to start with. And then everybody else, when it came out. I—" She hesitated, looking around nervously. But confession was proving a relief, and Joey was, after all, a stranger. She lowered her voice. "I'm still on probation. For stealing stuff. A whole gang of us, up in Portland where we used to live. It was supposed to be a lark, but it *wasn't!* It was awful! I was scared all the time."

There, the ghost was laid to rest. The girl drew a deep breath and the color returned to her cheeks. "I just wanted you to know how glad I am you locked that door! I mean it was really terribly important to me. Golly, my poor folks! You know, Dad changed jobs and they sold the house and—well, I don't know how much it cost them to move down here where I'd be with a different crowd of kids." She finished earnestly,

"Don't you ever believe stealing is an easy way to get stuff. I guess it's just about the most expensive way there is!"

"Yeh," Joey agreed, "I'll go along with that."

He was turning away when the girl asked curiously, "Say, aren't you on the track team? Wait a minute—" She groped for a name. "Oh, sure, you're Van, aren't you? I've seen you run. You're good."

Pleased but terribly embarrassed, Joey escaped. The warm glow of the girl's words went with him. It was nice to be recognized by a stranger—as Van. As a trackman. As a *good* trackman.

Much nicer, Joey admitted soberly, than being recognized as the kid who'd been picked up for shoplifting—or stealing cars—or breaking in someplace and smashing things. Yeh, a whole lot nicer!

Mr. Sanford was waiting for him when he left his last class that afternoon. "Joey, I just got a phone call with a message for you. One of the Guide Dog people happens to be in the area . . ."

Joey crossed his fingers. A wild, irrational hope flared inside him. *Here it comes; this is the miracle—*

"He'll be going through Westport tomorrow on his way back to San Rafael; he wants to take Eric along with him."

27

ooooooooo

JOEY STOOD MUTE. He couldn't summon up a single word, though his whole body ached with fierce denial. *No,* cried muscles and nerves and bones and bloodstream, *no, no,* NO!

Disturbed by the boy's absolute stillness, Mr. Sanford reminded him, "You know they much prefer transporting the dogs personally. Eric came by air because we're outside their regular delivery area. It's just a lucky chance they have someone coming through Westport at the time he's due to go back."

Continued silence from Joey.

"Well, it *is* much nicer for Eric," Mr. Sanford found himself saying defensively. "He'll enjoy the drive a lot more than being cooped in a plane cargo compartment!"

Still no response.

Mr. Sanford rallied his forces and said firmly, "So if you'll have the dog ready, Joey, before you leave for school tomorrow, the Guide Dog man will pick him up sometime during the morning."

It couldn't happen—but it had. The miracle had failed to appear. Final blow, Fate had even cut a week from Eric's stay. At the thought of all the things they'd planned to do that last week . . .

A humiliating sound rose in Joey's throat—like an animal struck down, frightened, in pain. He couldn't let it be heard. Tight-lipped, he turned and ran down the hall and out of the building.

By the time he reached home he had recovered his stoicism, along with a shred of stubborn hope.

"It's jus' too bad about this week," he told Eric as he combed and brushed the dog's shining coat. " 'Course we knew all along you'd have to go to San Rafael for a while—"

For a while. For a while. Just for a while.

"—but you'll come back, yessir, you better believe it! An' there'll be lots of time then to climb the butte. Anyway, *you* got to the top, didn't you, boy? I s'pose climbin' it again'd jus' bore you stiff—'specially if you didn't find another bear up there!"

Joey swallowed hard and gave Eric's coat a final needless smoothing down. "Now when this guy comes for you tomorrow, you be a good dog, remember—"

Only that was the trouble. Eric *would* be a good dog, always. Good, obedient, smart. His ears alert, his eyes bright, his complete attention focused on his teacher. Eric loved to learn; he loved feeling useful, important, responsible, with many duties to perform. Eric wouldn't fail at San Rafael . . .

Nor did Joey want him to fail.

"Oh, Eric, Eric," mourned Joey, and didn't care who looked out the window and saw him crouched there in tears, his arms around his dog. No stoic, he. Just a very human boy, facing up at last to the loss of a dearly loved companion.

Joey cut school the next morning. Nobody objected; Anna and Dirk, silently sympathetic, ignored the clock as though its tick-tick-tick was no more than a cricket's chirp. In midmorning the Guide Dog car pulled into the driveway. Joey tried to hate the man at the wheel—and couldn't. A true dog-man; Eric's response to his touch and voice proclaimed it instantly. He praised Eric, complimented Joey on his fine care, accepted the little bundle of Eric's cherished possessions, and listened seriously as Joey explained their value—

And was gone.

The house, the yard, became on the instant an echoing cavern of emptiness.

"Well," said Joey loudly, "guess I wasted enough time. Better get to school."

The reaction set in at Hopkins.

"So what if I flunk?" Joey jeered to himself as he squared away at the final test in science. "You think I care?"

He had been deprived of his miracle; all his efforts had been in vain. What difference now if his grades tumbled, if he was rude and sloppy and antagonized teachers and *Journal* customers, if he quarreled with Dirk and made Anna unhappy? Eric was gone.

"Alla stupid kids that leave their lockers open," Joey said recklessly, making his scowling way through the hall, "serve 'em right if I cleaned 'em out this week! Boy, I bet I could get me a summer's spendin' money outa this joint 'fore vacation!"

The Advanced Band was playing for the Hopkins graduation, but the Intermediate Band would have its chance to perform at an earlier ceremony, when the graduates took a thoughtful look back at their Hopkins years.

"Boy, will I give 'em something to remember!" Joey hooted. *Wham-bang-crash* . . . his drum would shake them up! So what if it cost him his place in Advanced Band next fall? *He* didn't care.

Eric was gone.

"Well, at last I've found a school sporting enough to take us on cross-country!" Mr. Dedham exulted. "It's out of season, of course. Won't count in the records. But Wilson Junior High has challenged Hopkins to a long-distance event!"

"Fuff," Joey told himself, "forget it. I'm sicka

runnin'. . . ." Eric was gone.

The gaping hole in Joey's life threatened to swallow him. Had he really spent all that time working with Eric, playing with him, thinking of him? His hours now rattled with emptiness.

Anna said, "Joey, how you have grown! Summer comes and nothing will fit, I know it. Now try everything on, this minute, you hear? So we see what to give away and what must be replaced."

"Sure," said Joey, not caring one way or another. Who cared if he wore jeans that showed his calves and shirts that split at the shoulder seams? Not he.

Eric was gone. . . .

But strangely, nothing worked out as he planned. He couldn't goof up the science test; a whopping lot of evening hours had gone into learning those facts; now he couldn't forget them.

His *Journal* customers depended on his service; after all, he'd sold most of them himself on its importance, hadn't he? So how could he let them down now? He couldn't.

When the band played for the graduates' goodbye, his hands took over the drumsticks with all the skill that had been patiently drilled into them and, disregarding his rebellious desire to disrupt the solemn ceremony, kept exactly on time.

And when he ran for Hopkins against the Wilson team, it made no difference that he didn't care about the outcome; habit took over and kept him jogging at a steady effortless pace, one foot before the other, on and on—till he crossed the finish line with no one else in sight, and there was Mr. Dedham hopping up and down like a kid, cheering him on to victory.

The truth was (reluctantly he had to admit it), he could no more revert to the stubborn, willful, wrong-headed Joey of last year than he could unteach Eric. While he had been training the dog, the dog had been training *him*—to punctuality, conscientious performance of duties, consideration of others, gentleness. The long months of working together, growing up together, had imprinted their pattern on both boy and dog. Indelibly.

Of all the empty days following Eric's departure, the Sunday that had been scheduled for the butte climb was surely the loneliest. Joey, his *Journal*s delivered, roamed about house and yard in a futile search for something to occupy mind and hands.

Bob didn't appear, but then Joey hadn't really expected him. After Eric's going, Bob had tried unusually hard to spare Joey's feelings, to think before he spoke, as though each word were a fragile egg that, once dropped, might splatter the whole countryside.

"Of course he'd stay away this Sunday," thought Joey. "Sure, he'd act like we hadn't planned a thing." Well, it was the thoughtful thing to do, but Joey, aching for activity, might almost have preferred the hurt of being reminded.

"Joey," Anna jogged his memory gently, "it grows warmer, and nothing done yet about your clothes . . ."

"Oh, yeh!" It was a relief to have something that needed doing. Joey made a full-scale campaign of it, emptying drawers and hangers, dragging boxes down from his closet shelf, till his bed was heaped high. Efficiently he created three piles—the will-do, the well-maybe, the gosh-no.

What came from the hangers fared best, but the things packed away in boxes—they were pretty funny, thought Joey, taking mild amusement in exposed inches of ankle and wrist. "Might just as well chuck 'em all out; no need to unpack the whole works."

Except that it gave him more to do.

And so, minutely, he examined and tried on every article in every box. And so, inevitably, he came upon something long forgotten . . .

Bob Barton's watch.

"Hully gee!" murmured Joey. He held the thin silvery disk on his palm; the cool metal stung hotter than a brand. "What'll I do with *this?*"

Impulse dictated that he get rid of it. Throw it away, anyplace, the farther the better. The boy who had secreted it, who had panicked in trying to collect the reward, was long gone now. Why should Joey be blamed for that boy's wrongdoings?

"I'll heave it out with the rubbish," said Joey in alarm. "I'll chuck it in the burning-pile. I'll—I'll—"

I'll give it back to Bob, said the new Joey. Eric's Joey.

He didn't know what he would say, didn't figure out any alibis or explanations . . . just pocketed the watch and started out for Bob's house.

The day was warm and windless, but nobody was on the game courts of the House. Joey parked his bike in the driveway and stood hesitantly, looking around. Did he have to go ring the bell, maybe face Bob's parents? He hadn't counted on that. Well, if he must . . .

On his way to the door Joey looked toward the duck pond, that spot of infamous memory . . .

And saw Bob, humped over on the bank. Bob hadn't seen Joey swish into the driveway. He didn't see his approach across the smooth-cropped green lawn.

"Hi," said Joey.

"Oh—hi," said Bob. He continued staring at the dipping and circling and quacking ducks.

If Joey had not been so concerned with his errand, he would have been puzzled by Bob's attitude. As it was, he plunged on single-mindedly. "I found this in my stuff—forgot all about it. It's yours, isn't it?"

Slowly Bob shifted his attention from the ducks to the extended disk. "Yeh," he said. Automatically he accepted it and strapped it on his wrist. Then surprise penetrated his absorption. "Hey, where'd *you* get it?"

"Found it at Hopkins, way back when."

"How come you kept it? Dad offered a reward."

"I dunno," Joey admitted. "I guess I was sore about somethin'."

"Yeh," Bob agreed, "you were always sore about somethin'—I dunno what."

"I don't know either." Odd, but that was the truth. Joey racked his brains and couldn't remember why he had been so hotly resentful of everything Bob did and said. A peculiar void made itself felt. Joey looked around, then asked, "Hey, where's Tex?"

Bob looked as though he had a sudden chill. Or an emotion too strong to conceal. "He's at the vet's. He had a heart attack."

"*Tex?*" Joey sat down suddenly beside Bob. "Aw, no!"

"Yeh," Bob took a deep breath. "All of a sudden last night he lifted his head an'—an' sort of tried to gulp in air like somethin' was chokin' him . . ."

Something was choking Bob. He couldn't go on. Joey felt a desperate need to give relief. "How is he now? Did you call?"

Bob nodded. "He's—they said he's resting easy."

"Well, then!" Unsuspected strength poured into Joey's veins, into his voice. "He'll be okay—just you wait and see! Gee, the stuff they got nowadays, pills an' shots an' all—sure, maybe he'll slow up a little, but so what? We don't have to climb *mountains* to have fun! A li'l ol' hike down the road an' back . . ."

Bob's eyes were on him as though he were Moses bringing down the sacred tablets. Joey said loudly, "Gosh, if *doctors* folded up like you, we'd be in a fine mess!"

"Yeh," agreed Bob. He managed a watered-down smile. "Guess I was kinda shook. You know, I can't even remember a time when there wasn't Tex—"

"Shucks, he'll be back!" Joey said heartily. "Makin' life tough for a whole lot of rabbits yet!" He felt that a change of subject was mandatory. Impulsively he confided his innermost secret ambition. "You know what? I'm gonna be a vet."

"You *are?*"

"Yep. Made up my mind while—while Eric was here. What's any better'n workin' with animals? Lots

207

of animals I like better'n lots of people."

"You bet! Me too." The sad droop went out of Bob's shoulders. He straightened, looking beyond the duck pond, the green lawns, the wide-branched trees. "Hey, that's a swell idea! Maybe we could have an office together."

"Why not?" The two boys sat side by side on the bank, joined by a powerful bond. "Funny," thought Joey, "he's really my very best friend!" Closer than anyone back home. How had it happened? With his old friends, he had shared endless hours of fun . . .

But with Bob he had shared sorrow, and that was the strongest tie of all.

Bob, remembering, said awkwardly, "I—I'll sure miss Eric. He was pretty great."

"Yeh," Joey acknowledged and dismissed the proffered sympathy quickly. *You don't get to keep anything*, he admitted; the truth was sad and blunt, but brought with it its own healing. *Nobody does, not even Bob. You just get to borrow it for a while.*

28

oooooooo

THE LETTER CAME on a bright, brisk November day. Seeing the postmark and the return address, Joey for a supercharged moment felt the wild thrumming of a hope long since put away.

He ripped open the envelope.

Guide Dogs for the Blind (the enclosed message read) would be happy to welcome Joey and his parents at a graduation ceremony to be held on Saturday of the coming week. A class of eight graduates, having completed twenty-eight days of intensive training, would be presented with Guide Dogs by the 4-H members who had raised the puppies in their homes.

A warmly personal postscript added: "Eric has been working with a young journalist, blinded in an accident. They have proved ideally suited to each other, as you will see for yourself if you can attend the graduation."

"Golly!" Joey rushed with his news to Dirk and Anna. "How about that?—takin' a newspaper man around to get his stories. Can't you jus' *see* him? Chasin' fire engines 'n' ambulances—prob'ly gettin' his picture in the paper!" Joey finished staunchly,

"Boy, they sure picked the best dog for the job! Bet they never had a dog at their kennels as smart an' quick an'—an' easy to get along with as Eric."

Above the boy's bobbing, excited head Dirk smiled at Anna. They were both very proud of the man emerging from this third son of theirs.

Dirk said, "I suppose you want to see this graduation?"

"Oh, yeh, sure." With equal readiness Joey would have expressed his desire to visit the moon and the unlikelihood of his getting there. "But I guess it'd be pretty expensive." Joey was very conscious of costs these days. After his announced ambition to become a veterinarian, Dirk had helped him figure the total he'd need for his education, and Joey was already saving toward it. Dirk, recognizing his serious intent, had returned the bank book and money jar, a gesture of good faith that made Joey feel six inches taller and twice as old.

Now Dirk cleared his throat. He said gruffly, "I will take you."

"*Huh?*" Joey stared at his father as at a friendly Martian, a being too unreal to be properly comprehended. "You *will?* Chee!" He tottered toward the phone to tell Bob the great news; then, remembering, came charging back. "Boy, thanks!"

They planned to drive to San Rafael the following Friday. Anna elected to remain at home. "*Na, na,* someone must water the plants and tend the furnace!" She waved them on their way with an inward welling of thanksgiving that they could go off like that, alone together, with no need of a buffer between them. To think that only a year ago the quarrel had divided father and son like a forbidding wall! Eric had brought the wall crashing down—yes, it was the good doggy, Anna had no doubt of it.

Nor did Dirk. As he drove southward Dirk reconsidered an idea that he had mulled over since Eric's departure. For Dirk it was a very revolutionary idea . . . "Anna will think I have lost my wits!" he grumbled to himself. But, yes, he would do it. The boy had earned it. And it would bring comfort after the ordeal ahead; presenting his beloved dog to a new master would not be easy.

Joey himself had no thought beyond seeing Eric again. Excitement buoyed him on a high wave of anticipation. "Boy, I bet he's a big guy now! . . . Just imagine all he musta learned! . . . Gee, d'you think he'll know us? . . . Bet nobody in that class is gettin' a handsomer dog than Eric!"

The last boast suddenly sobered him; until then he hadn't actually grasped the idea that Eric's new owner would never see what a handsome dog he had. "Blinded in an accident," the letter had said. That meant it was sudden. A young man with eyes as good as Joey's, going about a job that maybe he'd planned for as eagerly as Joey was planning *his* career—

And then, *whammo.* A black world, a black future. Joey shut his eyes tightly and tried to imagine groping his way down the road without sight to guide him. "*Golly!*" he murmured, and this time his exclamation was heart-shakingly fervent. "He sure needs Eric!"

It was a strange and touching "graduation."

Dirk had looked with vocal approval at the eleven-acre campus with its offices, kennels, students' dormitory; he had studied with a cattleman's interest the record on good work done here in selective breeding; he had been impressed by the training program ("Who pays?" he had asked, and marveled to hear that gifts alone sustained the school; the blind student paid nothing for dog or training or his month's stay on the campus).

But then came the actual graduation ceremony, and Dirk was as wordless, as heart-stirred, as Joey.

Together they watched the uncanny blending of man and dog into one smoothly performing unit. Moving with such confidence it was nearly impossible to believe him sightless, one hand lightly holding the U-shaped handle of his dog's harness, each student demonstrated his complete ability to go forward, to turn right or left, to stop at curbings and negotiate traffic, to detour obstacles, to avoid danger.

"There's Eric!" whispered Joey. "Oh, isn't he— isn't he—oh, *look* at him!"

Pride, responsibility, intelligence, all were in Eric's bearing as the handsome dog stepped out beside the thin, eager, smiling young man. Joey watched the man even more intently than the dog.

Yes . . . yes, they were good together; he could almost feel the communication that flashed between them. Something deeper than words, more intimate than tug on leash, an understanding of each other's needs that linked them closer than leash and harness ever could.

Not knowing that he did it, Joey reached out and gripped his father's hand. "Yeh," he said, the word deep and sure and full, in spite of the swelling that crowded his throat, "they'll get along swell!"

The formal presentation would come later, but with these words Joey gave Eric to the smiling stranger.

This is the moment, thought Dirk. *Yes, now I will tell him.* Aloud, he said, "It was good having a dog in the house. Perhaps when we get home, we should go back to one of those fancy kennels—the one with boxers, maybe?—and choose a puppy. Would you like that?"

213

Joey's startled eyes swerved from Eric to his father. "You mean it? Wow!" Then he looked back at the man with Eric. "Gee, that'd be great, only—what I been thinkin' was—well, is it all right if I take another Guide Dog puppy instead?"

Dirk echoed, "Another Guide Dog puppy?" Astonishment gave way to tender pride as he looked at the serious profile beside him and felt the hard grip of the boy's hand. So now it was eyes for the blind instead of a dog for Joey! "This is how you want it?"

"Yeh." Solemnly, Joey reviewed his decision and found it good. "Yes," he repeated firmly, "that's what I want to do."

HARPER TROPHY BOOKS
you will enjoy reading

HARPER & ROW, PUBLISHERS, INC.
10 East 53rd Street, New York, New York 10022